DELTA RED

Also by David Osborn

The Glass Tower

The French Decision

Love and Treason

Heads

Jessica and the Crocodile Knight (children)

Murder on Martha's Vineyard

Murder in the Napa Valley

Murder on the Chesapeake

The Last Pope

The Cape Cod Blue

A Cold Wind from the Andes

Alicia's Secret

The Head Hunters

Selected Reviews

The Last Pope

"A truly great novel. I plan to make it my finest motion picture."
> —Martin Poll, producer of *The Lion in Winter,* starring Peter O'Toole and Katharine Hepburn

"A thrilling blend of history, religion, and human relationships."
> —*The New York Post*

"Packs a powerful punch … reminiscent of the Shoes of the Fisherman …"
> —Booklist

The Glass Tower

"Breathless introduction to the inner workings of big business …"
> —*The Times* Literary Supplement

"A vivid, fast moving story about people in PR."
> —*SHE* magazine

"[An] institution story perfected by Zola and none the worse for it … deftly, excitingly told."
> —*The Daily Telegraph*

"A sharp and entertaining first from Mr. Osborn, who is already an accomplished screenwriter."
> —*Lincolnshire Evening Telegraph*

Murder on Martha's Vineyard

"A good tale of mystery and murder. Its plot twists and turns in and out of an intriguing whodunit that packs a punch at the end powerful enough to floor one."
        —*Western Morning News*

"This well-plotted thriller makes compulsive holiday reading."
        —*Salisbury Journal*

"This is the first entry in what might become a promising new series…. Osborn has created an interesting protagonist."
        —*Publishers Weekly*

"Before settling down to read this book, take the phone off the hook, make sure all the doors and windows are locked, set a large medicinal brandy within easy reach, and prepare to let David Osborn scare your pants off. Highly recommended."
        —*The Bloodhound*

"Delightful mystery is a zinger. Every one of its 258 pages says 'turn me.'"
        —*Chattanooga New Free Press*

Murder on the Chesapeake

"Satisfying tale … intrepid sleuth."
        —*Publishers Weekly*

"The tale is spun tightly and the main characters are engaging."
        —*Chicago Sun Times*

Open Season

"A truly brilliant novel ... an accomplished writer in all media, but ultimately a pro ... a superbly organized book, brutal, chilling, but carrying a terrible conviction."
—*Canberra Times*

"As commercial and exciting a novel as can be found today.... It is shocking, savage, and graphic, a cruel book that spares little in detail. There is unbearable suspense, headlong action, and ends with a final ironic twist that will leave the reader gasping. Osborn is a master storyteller and his remorseless style matches his remorseless narrative...."
—*Abilene Reporter News*

"David Osborn's story motif in *Open Season* is not new—the human set free to become the hunted, the quarry in a hunt made more exciting by the element of human intelligence and cunning on both sides. But Osborn who knows his way with a story and people and how to keep the suspense and relish boiling, gives it added spice and terror ... one of the season's top novels."
—*Waco* (Texas) *Tribune-Herald*

The French Decision

"Osborn's novel shrivels the nerves ... a gripping story skillfully developed ... the ironic epilogue [is] even more explosive."
—*Publishers Weekly*

"An exciting, highly plausible Washington thriller."
—Gore Vidal

"In a powerful story of industrial espionage which takes place in the United States and France, David Osborn examines American politics, the French economy, international high finance, and the Common Market as well as torture and love. He does it all with a gentle irony and without ever losing his perspective by deeply involving us in the troubled emotions of his hero, a young Arab posing as a Jew who takes American nationality to become a 'mole' in the service of French espionage...."
—*L'Express*, Paris

"An unforgettable thriller of high-level intrigue ... this fictional world, vividly portrayed, is just realistic enough to be disturbing and unsettling.... Aaron Zeismann a real, brilliantly conceived character ... the climax of this flawlessly plotted story is stunning, as is its ironic epilogue. Anyone will find this thriller impossible to put down...."
—*Pittsburgh Press*

DELTA RED

DELTA RED

A novel by

David Osborn

DAGMAR
MIURA
LOS ANGELES

Published by Dagmar Miura
Los Angeles
www.dagmarmiura.com

Delta Red

First published 2018

ISBN: 978-1-942267-56-0

for Robin, Raphaella, and Sebastian,
with love

ONE

Hello, my name is Kasie Sanders, and no, Kasie isn't short for anything, it's what they gave me thirty-five years ago when I was born in Ann Arbor, Michigan, and was my grandmother's name, and God knows where she got it. It didn't fit with her being a full-bloodied Osage who had the temerity to defy tribal elders and marry a man of Scottish-German descent. Hence I'm an Osage mix, only to a small extent I know, but proud of it.

This story really isn't so much about me. It's about a small part of a widespread federal investigation into sex crimes in general and into one hideous crime in particular that resulted from an unknown cyberspace geek hacking into emails in which the most obscure phrase imaginable attracted the attention of a *New York Times* investigative reporter who wasn't even investigating sex crimes.

Part of that small part of the FBI investigation was played by me, of all people. I was picked out of the blue to play it, and I wouldn't say my role was fraught from beginning to end with danger—a lot of investigating is seemingly unrelated to what or who is being investigated and isn't fraught with anything except seemingly unrelated hard work and thinking—but there were moments, nevertheless, when I confess I wished I was elsewhere.

How was it I got picked? Well, I have to go way back before it happened in order to show why I apparently qualified, and I have to introduce you to the team investigating, and how they got involved and dragged me in, so bear with me.

I don't remember much about Ann Arbor because when I was three we moved to a rural area in Arkansas where my grandparents had roots. My father, a professor of European history at the University of Michigan, had inherited a dairy farm from his father near the town of Delaney, which is close by the White River and a short distance north of the Ozark National Forest. He had spent much of his youth on the farm and had the life-style associated with dairy cows in his blood. He'd always secretly wanted to own and operate one and couldn't resist his inheritance, so with Mom's full approval—she was a social anthropologist—that was where we went.

My childhood was in many ways idyllic. How could life on a dairy farm, although hard work, be anything but? Memories of it are seared in me: Dad's cheerful singing as he brought in our herd evenings to be milked, my mother in her apron on the porch of the wonderful old farm house mixing something in a bowl, my little sister Arielle cheerfully swinging back and forth in the tire Dad had hung by a rope from the branch of a big old maple tree that shaded the front yard.

Dad and Mom were mannered people and brought me up to be like them. But when I was only nineteen and for reasons that still to this day defy me, I rebelled against it, along with all the security and love it stood for, and, to the consternation of my parents, left home. All I can remember of my emotions of the time was that I had some sort of irresistible compulsion to seek something different, to be on my own and do my own thing, although what that "thing" could be I had no idea, nor why I became unreasonably angry, as though my very life was threatened, if anyone disputed my right to lead it in whatever manner or wherever I chose.

I left home in a storm, and the ensuing four years found me living with Jordie, a clarinet player whose ambition was to play with one of the Dixieland bands in the famed French Quarter of New Orleans. Unfortunately, his ambitions didn't work out, he fell into drugs, and our match ended with rage and abuse—it was all my fault, he said—and finally, one awful night, he really went for me, and I dialed 911.

The cops came. One in particular was a lady cop. She took me to the emergency room, where they fixed a broken nose and other results of the battering, and then on to the shelter. Emotionally, I was at rock bottom. And depressed beyond description. I kept thinking of how low I'd sunk from the idyllic home I had so foolishly left behind. I'd defeated myself, there was nobody to blame but me, and I think more than anything I was broken-hearted that there was no longer any dream left of "whatever" to cling to, no longer any freedom to be brilliant in. I got to where I thought of suicide.

But I didn't because of that lady cop. She saved my life. She didn't believe that help ended with rescuing me from being worked over by Jordie. She kept coming to see me in the nasty little fur-nished room I was living in and encouraging me and even a few times helped me out with money. No, she didn't have any ulterior motives, she wasn't religious, she wasn't gay or anything like that.

Incredibly, she was just someone who cared.

I will always remember what she said when I asked her why she'd become a cop. She thought a moment and said, "I'd got a little down in life, like you, and needed a job. The police were recruiting and I thought, hell, why not, and went for it, mostly because there was so much misery and unhappiness everywhere, so many people living without, that I saw the police as a way to help people even if it meant getting gangs and crime off their backs so they could live in peace."

That did it for me. Being a police officer seemed solidly dependable and a way back to sanity, so like her, I said to myself, *why not,* and with her help joined up myself. I went to training and learned the ropes, all the things a cop has to do and all he or she has to know about laws and people's rights, how a true cop is being much more than arresting people, that a cop should represent civic decency and respect. All that, while every minute a little numb, it was all so strange. I felt this wasn't really my niche in life, but to my surprise, after a while I found I liked it, especially investigative work, when I was promoted to detective. It wasn't the farm in Arkansas, but it was home just the same.

Until it all abruptly came crashing down, with my shooting the guy holding up a store when answering a 911 and getting accused of murder by a really nasty district attorney and, even though supported by most of my fellow cops and a lot of community leaders, I had to forcibly retire from the force, which in plain English means I was fired. I spent weeks in hell with the only upside my parents, who were told what was happening by my lawyer and came to New Orleans to stand by me. I learned a lot from that, most of all how to swallow pride, how to say I'm sorry, how to return no-strings love.

But I still had enough pride left to want to stand on my own two feet. I had no place to go, however, except to use my knowledge of photography I'd learned way back in community college in Little Rock after I'd left the farm. So I established myself in the area I'd got to know, which included Baton Rouge, taking pictures of weddings and kids' parties. And hated it, but it was the only way I could think to make a living. For me, it was a big step backward. I missed my police job, I missed the camaraderie I'd had with many of my fellow officers and being a help to ordinary people, some in trouble of their own making, some troubled by others. I missed investigative work in every aspect, and above all I missed being somebody who counted, even if only in a small way.

But photography fed me and paid the rent, and so that's what I was doing one late-spring day when the humidity was unbearable, and on a day and at a wedding when, unknown to me, this story began.

I was photographing in a New Orleans suburb, and my work and my subject was being menaced by a thunderstorm that would almost surely sweep up across the delta from the Gulf, but hopefully not before bride and groom had gone off into their new life together and all their guests had dispersed.

As I rushed about the reception taking pictures, and when I shot the bride throwing her bouquet to her maid of honor, I was totally unaware of a conversation between two men in faraway Washington, D.C., nor that something important was unravelling, nor that sooner than I could imagine that "something" would bring on a complete change in my life and set me on a whole new course, as far from shooting pictures at weddings and kids' parties as you could imagine.

Here's what I eventually learned that the two men said to each other, and from a man my father's age who was to loom so importantly in my life. What the phone call that one of the Washington men made to him in Baton Rouge was about, and why it was important, I didn't learn until much later, when he told me all the details. It was the first step for me, of all people—a wedding photographer and a disgraced ex-cop—getting picked for the job.

TWO

Around mid-morning of that very day, while I photographed the wedding, the two men I mentioned were seated in a small brightly-lit office high in the Hoover Building that looked down over the Capitol's Pennsylvania Avenue. One, Perry Chung, I was to learn, was the Asian-American investigative reporter for the *New York Times* who was currently looking into civil rights violations in some of the Southern states where there were reports of immigrant workers given fake green cards so they could replace Americans in factory jobs at far less than minimum wage.

It had taken him a while to get there. It was unseasonably hot, the cherry trees were fast losing their earlier blossoms, and when Uber failed him and he couldn't find a regular taxi, he'd walked from Union Street station after taking an early Amtrak down from New York. He was still feeling the outdoor heat and was in his shirtsleeves, his jacket hung over the back of his chair.

The other man, I was told, was George J. Bishop, a mid-level FBI executive in the criminal division who was one of a sizeable team investigating a suspected sex trafficking ring in the United States and its connection to organizations in Malaysia and Thailand.

Bishop studied Chung. In contrast to his own relatively sturdy ebony skin and bearded appearance, Chung was a slender, scholastic-looking man with middle-age balding, a pale face with a continuously haunted expression, and a solid reputation. Chung stared back at him with bland eyes.

The conversation between the two men went like this. "Perry, what's your source for this?" That was Bishop.

"Come off it, George. You know I don't reveal my sources. But for what it's worth, you can take what he picked up as accurate. Nobody made it up. The guy could hack into Vladimir's emails in five seconds if he got that into his head." That was Chung.

It wasn't the first time that the reporter had keyed the FBI into something of possible interest to the agency, and Chung had never played false.

There was no reason to dismiss what the *Times* reporter revealed now, Bishop thought. He found himself fighting back resentment of what might turn out to be dull, detailed, and frustrating work and particularly, because of it, that he had been assigned to a job in the Bureau that had forced him into investigating the sordidness of pedophilia. There were times when another minute of involvement in such filth made him want to pack in twenty years of successful career in a job and place he loved and go somewhere else where sex crimes didn't exist. Any place.

He said, "I didn't mean to seem to doubt you, Perry. I'm sure your source is reliable. But Warriner, the Delta Red guy? Shit, man, he's one of the most revered figures in Southern politics."

Chung laughed. "Hold on, George. I don't mean the former governor. He's now over the hill—gaga, I heard. The emails are from his son, Connors Warriner Junior."

"The congressman, right?"

"Right. He took over Delta Red when the old man fell into Alzheimer's."

"And we *are* talking about the hot sauce?"

"Delta Red. Right again. Apparently he's is just as down on civil rights as the old man was. The KKK and Nationalists love him. Breitbart News is a big fan. Wrote him up recently as upcoming presidential material the American people could believe in. Can you beat it? And we weren't, mind you, even on to *him.* We were covering Reb Bannerman."

"B&R Foods?" Bishop again didn't hide surprise.

"Correct. If I'm right, he lost his seat in the Louisiana senate three years ago in a fraud case. Barely missed a jail sentence. He's been secretly negotiating a possible takeover of Delta Red by his grocery giant. That's one reason for the emails to him from Warriner Junior."

Bishop looked down at a printout Chung had given him. "Who's this Amelie Faure? You've got emails here to her from both Connors Junior and Bannerman."

"You don't know about Amelie?" Chung was faintly amused. It wasn't unusual to find his newspaper one up on law enforcement agencies, even the FBI, that were dedicated to the same area of crime he had information on. "I thought you guys were into everything rancid," he said. "She's the famous New Orleans celebrity madam, mid-sixties with a twenty-one-year-old figure, a glamorous, overly made-up face, and enough jewelry decorating top-price designer dresses to open a jewelry boutique. She's been billed as running a five figure per date escort service."

"And getting away with it?"

Chung said, "Cops down there tell me half her clients run the state, the current governor among them."

"And you suspect her of involvement with pedophiles, too?"

Chung laughed. "I don't suspect her of anything. I'm investigating civil rights violations. Pedophilia along with human trafficking, and you're welcome to both, is your department. But when you're in the sex trade for years like Amelie, I should think you might be into almost anything."

Bishop didn't reply. He stared thoughtfully at the printout of emails Chung had given him. Then, reading from it, he said, "looking forward to one of her girls to be." He glanced back up at Chung. "Girls meaning someone not yet grown up? That's cutting it pretty slim, Perry, to say that might indicate pedophilia. *Girls* is a term commonly applied to a lot of whores."

"I agree," Chung replied. "It could only mean some new talent Amelie is planning to add to her string of regulars. Except when Connors says it in two emails running, it maybe hints at obsession. In my book at least. I don't cater to the escort business, and I know you don't either, but suppose we both did. Can you imagine email salivating to this extent over just another night's lay with some unfortunate hooker who thinks that's the way to fame and fortune?"

"Yeah, maybe …" Bishop agreed, "Jesus, what the hell goes on nowadays? Used to be stupid hard-up johns who only saw women for sex. Now its sickos and whips and children and God only knows what." He sighed resignedly and shook his head. "Okay, Perry, we'll check it out. And thanks. Lunch?"

"Love to, but I'm basically here to indulge with some stupid senator." Chung grinned. "He hates the media. Thinks we're a vast conspiracy. Wish me luck."

When Perry Chung had gone, Bishop thought for a minute. What he hadn't told Chung was that the New Orleans vice squad had also sent him a couple of Amelie Faure's emails that they'd nailed. Two were to hotels in Bangkok and Kuala Lumpur—Thailand and Malaysia—enquiring about reservations for a vacation visit. A third was to an Englishman, one Clarence Hart-Bromley, a long-time resident of Kuala Lumpur and suspected of being a key figure in illegal sex trafficking, including pedophilia.

George Bishop felt a sudden surge of unexpected interest. Perhaps pursuing what his old friend Perry Chung had brought him wouldn't turn out to be dullness exemplified after all. He swung round his laptop and brought up a database where he found Faure's name, then Connors Warriner Junior's. He read what was there, which wasn't much other than corruption, went to lunch in the Hoover Building's cafeteria, and had a hamburger and a coffee. When he came back, and since Warriner Junior lived in the Baton Rough area, he put in a call to Jermyn Gutierrez, the agent in charge of the criminal investigation division at the FBI office there. He reported on his meeting with Chung and said, "Hate to have the *New York Times* top us, but I've been dealing with Chung for years now. He's reliability itself. Can you get out a warrant to monitor the emails?"

"Warriner's?"

"Both of them. Bannerman's, too."

"George, 'girls to be' is probably not enough stuff to get a warrant on. Not with today's court system down here. Rousing the ire of either Warriner or Bannerman could prove fatal if it ever got out, and leaking confidential information even with the courts seems par for the course these days. After the appellate being overruled on the voting rights verdict last year, even the lower court judges are being super cautious. And if we succeeded, I still don't see any guarantee in monitoring the guy's mail and coming up in spades. If either Warriner or Bannerman are actually up to no good, the phrase used in your emails is wariness personified. Catch one unlucky fish, we say in Louisiana, doesn't mean you'll go on to catch a whole school."

"What do you suggest?"

"Not sure. Maybe a plant?"

"On Amelie Faure?"

"No. She'd sniff it right away. You don't stay in her business for twenty-five years and get caught.

So it would be on Connors Warriner Junior for a start. Bannerman is smart as hell, but I hear the congressman isn't. Big-deal full of himself, but no Phi Beta. In fact, the supposed negotiations for a B&R Foods takeover of Delta Red, which is all hush-hush, is mostly being done on his behalf, or behind his back, by one Fredericka Mayworth, the Warriner family's business manager. Clever-assed, Harvard Law School and Wharton MBA lady. The whole crowd sucks, so I suppose undercover is worth the try even if a long shot."

"Wouldn't planting someone in his office be near impossible? He only staffs about six plus an intern. And none of them are grade-A stupid."

"I wasn't thinking of his office."

"Oh?"

"I was thinking of his home."

"His home? That sounds even trickier."

"Yes. But it might not be. Let me think on it a bit."

"Well, you're down there, Jermyn. I'm not. I'll fax you copies of the emails."

"Thanks. I'd like to see them."

"And Jermyn, if you go for a plant, put the right person on the job, okay? It may be nothing, but if we had luck and it brought out even a slight lead to that gang in Malaysia and Thailand, it could turn up a biggie, and we don't want a fuck-up. The chief had enough trouble with the mess the San

Francisco office got him into on the election hacking stuff last year, okay?"

"I'll keep you posted."

When they'd hung up, Jermyn Gutierrez, the agent in Baton Rouge, shifted uneasily in his big office chair. He was close to retirement and fighting a lifelong weight problem, and it was hot and the air conditioning in the FBI's new ultramodern building not functioning a hundred percent. *Typical,* he thought. *Brand new and it's already taking time off.* Worse than the heat, was his feeling mildly depressed? Driving to work that morning, he'd aroused the ire of another motorist when he'd accidentally come close to cutting him off, and the motorist had wasted no time in cursing him out. "Bloody Mexican asshole, go back to your own goddamned country."

What the hell did he have to do, Gutierrez wondered. Wear a blond wig and hang a card around his neck that said, "I'm a U.S. citizen?" Would stupid rednecks like that guy ever accept anyone who was brown, which to them was as bad, if not even worse, than being black?

He pulled a tissue from a box on his clean-swept desk and wiped the dampness from his forehead where it wasn't half covered with straight dark hair that belied his age and forty years of government service, had a slug of iced tea he'd had picked up for him by the young intern assigned for the summer to be his administrative assistant, pitched the empty can in the waste basket, and then swung around to stare out at a tailored lawn through the floor-to-ceiling glass that was one wall of his immaculately kept modern office. The limpness of the American flag suspended from atop the lawn's tall white flag pole testified to what sort of a day it was.

He found himself wondering. *Why*? Why, if Mayworth was handling the possible takeover, was Connors mailing and texting Bannerman at all? The thought seemed almost to confirm Bishop's suspicions. And men using so-called escort services, especially the married ones, usually kept their doing so strictly to themselves unless there was something special going on they could safely share. The thought gave him a glimmer of hope that his Washington colleague might actually be on to something. He'd never known Bishop to show interest in false leads, and he'd seen him turn up big cases on even less evidence than a vague and possibly innocent email. But leave it to a *New York Times* investigative journalist to drive them both nuts with a case that might prove, on the other hand, to be a long haul to nothing.

Experience had taught Gutierrez not to act hastily, and furthermore always to cover himself. An hour later he was seated at the conference table on the floor above his office along with three other seasoned agents: Tom Whitman, his boss and the still youthful deputy director of the Baton Rouge Agency, who was black and to whom, in spite of a master's degree in criminology, caution was not necessarily always a requirement; Amos Salt, the agencies forensic specialist, a scientific PhD who tended to be just the opposite and Sally Putnam, the Baton Rouge Bureau's communications director, an attractive but steely younger woman who'd come to the FBI with a Yale law degree.

"I don't think 'girls to be' is enough to bring the guy in for questioning," he'd told them right away. "We'd end up on the wrong end of a law suit."

That had been at once agreed to by everyone. The consensus was also that going undercover with someone in his New Orleans congressional office would be nigh impossible. Connors Warriner Junior had never been known to employ anyone except a close friend of a close friend or the offspring of someone close, preferably a relative. With the congressman it was forever secrecy and keeping it close to his vest.

The congressman's home was at Lonsdale Hall, a famed plantation house that had been in his family for more than six generations. The historically classic antebellum property was on the Bayou Teche, the long sluggish waterway, once the course of the Mississippi, that ran down from Port Barre to the Atchefalaya River Delta on the Gulf. When Gutierrez suggested putting an undercover agent into the house itself, Salt, an easy laid-back man in his sixties and like Gutierrez soon to retire, was negative on the idea, even though he was one who always looked for alternatives. "Jesus, Jermyn, that's taking a hell of a risk," he said. "Why not just bug the whole place instead?"

Sally Putnam was skeptical about bugging. "We can do it, sure," she said, a trifle sarcastic as well as with a touch of irony. "Send in a crowd of electricians and plumbers on some sort of excuse and hopefully not wise up anyone, okay, but seeking your evidence, if any, would only end up audio, and suppose what you're looking for was visual. So zero, no?"

"She's right," Whitman said. "With all due respect, Amos, we'll skip the onsite bugging. Email surveillance instead would be better and less expensive. And I suggest we try to get an order to continue that. Given the current lack of judges, it will take time, however, so in the meanwhile, what else? An outside listening device? But that's still just audio. Besides, what about overriding household chatter? It could take months to sort the wheat from the chaff." He pushed away an ice coffee he had finished and leaned forward, resting both elbows on the table. "So let's think once more about a plant. Where would we be looking, and for what? The *for what* is simple. *Where* is damned near the universe itself: photographs, letters, overheard conversations or audio recordings, laptops, thumb drives, iPhones, old tapes or CDs, even some other at-the-moment nameless physical object that could be incriminating. Finally, and at best, personality traits that would possibly point to this sort of crime."

Amos Salt said, "Given all that, and if we do decide on a plant, then we come down to a different question. Not where or what but *who*."

"Definitely agreed," Sally Putnam said. "We're not just talking about invading a house, we're talking about invading a family, and for all we know, one of which is suspect of being a criminal and possibly has ties to the lethal pros in Asia. And those guys don't play by anybody's rules."

"Check," Tom Whitman said. "For one lousy pedophile, even a bloody congressman in our midst, if he indeed is such a secret horror, I wouldn't consider wasting resources and time with any of this. Except finding one rat in your cellar can often lead to your finding a whole damned passel of them. If our getting into this might possibly—just possibly, because it's the slimmest of slim chances—help the guys trying to nail any of the bastards behind organized sex trafficking, well then …" He broke off, his thought unfinished, and turned to Jermyn Gutierrez, who up to this point had remained silent. "Jermyn, What do you think?"

"Personality, Tom," Gutierrez said, not answering Whitman's unfinished thought directly. "Personality and type. If we do go in, we can't go in with your ordinary guy, if a guy at all. Sally just nailed it when she said we're invading a family. It has to be someone who would fit in naturally. Let's remember whom we are dealing with. They are rich and socially prominent besides being hard-nose powerful. And, on top of all that, I suspect rather a tight-knit clique unto themselves. They're not people to easily accept a stranger in their midst."

"How many of them are they?" Salt asked.

"Six in the family plus a social secretary, a business manager who is there most of the time—has an office and her own bedroom—and seven live-in servants. A small crew of gardeners have quarters on the property, while any other outdoor labor comes in by the day through a landscape agency."

"Plant an eighth servant?" Amos asked.

"I doubt the family would have any reason for hiring an additional," Gutierrez said. "They're already outnumbered."

There was a silence. Whitman looked at the others who looked back, waiting. Without thinking, he slowly crunched a big fist around his empty plastic coffee container, leaving it bent double. A minute passed. Then he said, "Okay, guys. Play undercover? I'll go for it. Everything points that way. We put someone in Lonsdale Hall, but as Amos said, and we all agreed, who? Jermyn, I'll leave that up to you. When you find our plant, pass them by me for approval, okay? If I agree to them, I'll take responsibility if they screw up."

Gutierrez went back down to his office, sat silently for a while at his desk, and then, cursing pedophiles in general and Connors Warriner Junior in particular, if he indeed was one, he pulled a printed roster of names from a desk drawer. On it were the twenty-one agents under him in the Baton Rouge criminal investigation unit. He checked down through them carefully. Seventeen were men and four were women. In his imagination, he matched the name of each to the face and personality he knew. Then, putting the roster back in his desk drawer, he rolled his chair away from his desk, mentally setting one agent after another into Lonsdale Hall. As he carefully reviewed them, not one seemed to fit either the house or the family that lived there. Each was either too old or too rough and ready, was not smart enough, or wouldn't fit the social elitism of the Warriner family. Each, also, was simply the kind of person who might arouse suspicion or, to his thinking, be not flexible enough in basic makeup as to be able to assume totally an entirely new identity or character. With one man after another eliminated, he turned to the women. Reviewing each one in the same way he had reviewed the men, he felt none of them qualified either.

Dead end. Gutierrez stared a last moment or two at his list of agents, and then as he put it back in his drawer, a thought suddenly struck him. Did whomever it would be have to be FBI? Could he not recruit and deputize an outsider? Although that, too, on second thought, might turn up nobody. Besides, he couldn't even think of where to start looking. He didn't know that many people—a few neighbors, a handful of relatives, and an occasional good friend. He'd been too hard at work for too long to build much of a social acquaintance, and he could hardly advertise—"FBI needs outside undercover agent." He had connections with both the New Orleans and the Baton Rouge police, as well as with the state police force, but ruled out all three. Casting a broad net would totally jeopardize security and the utter secrecy necessary when going undercover.

He lumbered to his feet and circled his wide clean-swept desk to stand staring out the window at the heat-soaked lawn and the flag hanging limply from the tall flagpole. He'd already had it for the day, and there were still numerous things on his calendar to take care of before he could pack it in. Bloody Washington. Why the hell did they have to go and dump this on him and all on the say-so of a newspaper guy who wasn't even into criminal investigation? A man could only do so much in one day. Chasing up someone to help hunt down a pedophile would have to wait.

And then he suddenly thought of someone, and a cover he could use for them.

THREE

And, of course, that someone was me.

He only had seen me once or twice, and usually at a distance—we lived in the same neighborhood and used the same gym for weekly workouts—but working on a hunch and with his years of experience observing people, he'd gone and read up on me in old back newspapers. Afterward, he'd researched my whole life other than my stint as a police officer. He knew more about me than I did about myself.

He even knew that my current home which was fairly close to his and was in a complex on the west bank of the Mississippi, just south of Port Allen. It was a small one bedroom apartment overlooking the river that I shared with Alysia, a tall dark-skinned girl with a wild afro and a crazy sense of humor to match, whom I liked a lot and who worked in town for the IRS and was detailed to catch tax evaders. We'd really nested into the place, had decorated it together to our mutual taste, and felt as though ever moving out would be a disaster.

That same week then, and I guess a few days later, found me doing the same old thing to make a living—photographing a wedding in New Orleans where for hours I lugged around videos and a tri-pod and my still camera, an expensive top-of-the-line Canon, and wished I wasn't. Weddings kept reminding me of my own unmarried state, the end-less loneliness of the single woman past thirty-five when all of a sudden, unless you were glamorous beyond your own poor appearance, you weren't even in demand as an extra. Affairs, sure. I enjoy sex as much as nearly anybody, and what girl doesn't have her share. But I hadn't yet found the guy with whom I wanted to join up with in paying bills and sharing friends and life in general, as well as bed, for all the years ahead, and even though I was still more or less pretty at thirty-five, the chances of Mr. Right appearing in my life were ever getting less by the day.

I hadn't given up, though. I did the best I could with my appearance. The ugly scar across my fore-head where I'd been whipped with the barrel of a

Glock automatic in that holdup mess when I was a cop had been erased with plastic surgery courtesy of a citizens support group. I didn't go for much makeup, although I probably should have. I used a little mascara and no lipstick. I try to eat wisely and have managed to keep the same figure—well, pretty much so—that I had at twenty-five.

That particular wedding on that particular day was an afternoon affair, and after the ceremony in the church, the reception, in the ball room of a convention center fifteen minutes away, seemed to last forever. It was well past eight o'clock when I was able to finally leave and set my GPS for home, which was a good two hours away at best.

And, of course, I hit the worst. Getting out of New Orleans was murder, the traffic impossibly heavy, and it was no better when I finally was able to get off the toll causeway across Lake Pontchartrain and onto Interstate 10, where my vain hopes were dashed by an equally dense stream of cars and the driving made even worse by the awaited thunderstorm and heavy rain that obliterated a week of clear-blue skies and an almost unbearable, humid-intense heat.

The drive had jagged me up with a nervousness I couldn't identify. Alysia had left a note saying she was out on a date with some television guy, and after putting back a Kool-Aid and getting out of my work clothes, I decided to go to the gym. A half hour on the elliptical was usually the cure for any ill feeling. The gym was only a short distance away. The rain had let up, and I walked it in few minutes and found it nearly empty, its scores of idle machines like somber sleeping robots. I nodded at several of the regulars, got on the elliptical, turned on the TV panel to see if there was still a Planet Earth, and went to work.

The exercise routine left me, as usual, with a mind empty of thought except to get home, have a good long shower and get to bed with a book. Currently I was puzzling out Kafka. Tomorrow was Sunday; I could sleep late, and then I'd be kept more than incredibly busy developing and printing film in the small basement storeroom I rented and had converted into a photography darkroom, where bottles of developing solution lined shelves and a big enlarger occupied one end of a long work table. You can shoot great pictures with an iPhone or an iPad, but wedding shots—and I had taken hundreds—require more because of what you have to do to the pictures afterward to make them perfect.

My thoughts on only that, I was jarred back into

reality by a quiet voice demanding my attention.

"Miss? Miss Sanders, could I have a quick word with you?"

I found myself confronted at the door out of the gym by a stocky, overweight, and older fatherly-type man, a Latino whose straight black hair was without a hint of gray. I vaguely recognized him as one of the regulars.

He said, apologetically, "I see you here occasionally, so perhaps you'll excuse my lack of formality. My name is Gutierrez. Jermyn Gutierrez." Even as he spoke he produced a wallet and flipped it open, and I found myself with something of a shock looking at the identification of an FBI agent.

For a moment it didn't register, and then it did, and taken back, I fumbled for something to say, and could only blurt out, "Sorry?"

He smiled at me. "Please don't be alarmed. I'm too old to come on to young ladies, I assure you. I wanted to talk to you professionally. I know you are busy as a photographer, but could you possibly spare me a few minutes during the week at my office? It would be strictly on a professional basis."

When still completely surprised and a little confused I remained silent, he said, "I'm not mistaken? You are Kasie Sanders, aren't you? Once a detective with the New Orleans police? All that bodega shooting a few years ago with the murder charge against you?"

I felt a sudden stab of fear. Real fear that was like icy fingers clutching at every part of my insides. And thought, *What in the name of God is this all about?* Was it all going to come back at me, the whole damn mess I'd somehow managed to bury so I could get on with life?

I found my voice. "Yes," I said. "I am."

FOUR

I saw him, as arranged, on Monday, a wet-damp day when the heat had broken a little with the weekend thunderstorms, but the sky was still overcast. He hadn't said why he wanted to see me, and I still had no idea why I'd agreed to, except to think that I had information about someone or something while a cop that the FBI wanted to ask me about. It seemed almost obligatory to help them if I could. Once in law enforcement, you sort of always are, regardless.

Presenting myself at the front desk, I showed my driver's license as identification, and as I was scrutinized by a tough woman agent in a blue skirt and white blouse who had a revolver strapped to her hip, I suddenly felt my fears well up again, and an attack of nervousness that went with regret at my having come. I'd forgotten what it was like to be under the thumb of officialdom.

When I was announced, there was what seemed a forever silence, and then finally I heard Jermyn Gutierrez's voice come back, and I could see his face on a small security screen lodged on one corner of toughie's desk. "Send her right up," he said.

I didn't realize then that his meeting me the previous night was hardly impromptu. He'd been secretly observing me in the gym and elsewhere over the past ten days and, used to seeing me in gym clothes, almost didn't recognize me in a light-blue, designer sun dress I occasionally wore and with my neck-length and straight dark hair, for once blown tidy and not in a ponytail. He told me later he'd hesitated at telling reception to send me up because I looked more a teenager than an ex-cop, and for a moment he'd thought that somehow there'd been a mix-up.

When his order came through to the desk, I was at once escorted to the elevator by a silent young man in a dark business suit, the jacket of which barely hid a .45 strapped to his waist and whom I hadn't noticed. FBI agents tend to be invisible. When we arrived three floors up, I was accompanied by him down a brightly lit hall to Gutierrez's spacious office, where Gutierrez rose at once from behind his desk to wave at the young man to pull up a chair for me, and ordered him to bring two coffees. "Sugar and half-and-half for me," and, turning to me, "The same for you, or do you drink it black?"

I said, "Black's fine, thank you," and as the young man hastened out, tried to think, as I had most of the night and while getting dressed that morning to drive to the Baton Rouge FBI headquarters, what it might be that I knew that they might want to be informed of. Trying desperately to remember everything of possible importance through the years I'd spent as a cop, I could think of nothing. Why on earth, when meeting him at the gym, hadn't I asked then? I'd been caught so flat-footed that at the time all I'd been able to think was that the FBI was so all powerful and, in my books, so close to sacrosanct that you didn't ask them questions. They asked you.

I waited and, as I remember, defensively prim with my hands folded ladylike on my lap while Gutierrez shuffled some papers from a file on his desk, and then, holding them up for me to see, said, "Your New Orleans police file. Before we talk, I wanted to brief myself on a number of things." He put the papers down. "But first: my calling you in is strictly confidential, Miss Sanders. Can the FBI count on you for that?"

Completely surprised, I eyed the papers. There

were pictures of me among them. I saw, one looking trim and proud in my police uniform and looking so different from the way I looked today. And
there were news clippings as well, with every detail
of the scandal of my shooting the guy and being
ultimately fired from my police job and being put
on trial for murder. And all the lies of the smug
politically appointed prosecutor.

Wanting to know why he'd got hold of my files
and what I was doing there became stronger than
ever, but I thought, *Don't ask him why, wait for him
to tell you.* So I answered just, "Yes, sir."

Gutierrez said nothing. He silently studied me,
and I instinctively knew what he was thinking. I had
changed over the years since the murder charge. I
didn't look at all the same woman he'd seen in endless news photos at the time and on television. He
almost hadn't recognized me as time had virtually
obliterated the face he and half the country had
seen almost daily when reporters had indulged in a
field day with my private life. There was one I particularly loathed who insisted I didn't fit being a cop
and wrote that there was too much of the maverick
in me and marching to my own drummer to be a
good law-enforcement officer. And just because I
kept my mouth shut and tried to hang on to the
little dignity I had left during all the court proceed-
ings, there was another who had wondered where
I'd got the idea to act like I had "class" while just a

cop, when I never ever had any such idea.

Gutierrez broke the silence. He said, "You came to New Orleans thirteen years ago from Arkansas, is that right?"

It again brought my thinking up short. I said, "Yes, sir. Fourteen, actually," and wondered again where all this was going. There was everything about me in the file he'd been studying, why did he bother to ask me?

"Why New Orleans?" he asked.

"Personal reasons, sir." I wasn't about to let him in on the Jordie saga, no matter what. And he probably knew all about it anyway.

Gutierrez grunted. "Fair enough, I guess. But then why police work? You have a degree in photography from a good community college."

By now, I was beginning to relax a little, certain I wasn't in some sort of trouble, but just the same I wasn't going to tell him either that becoming a cop at first was just an escape from that dark moment that now was slowly fading from memory. I said evasively, "Why does anybody?"

Gutierrez pushed aside the file. He said, "Miss Sanders, your record with the New Orleans police prior to the unfortunate bodega incident was outstanding. In your first year you won the police marksmanship contest and your work in the detective squad virtually made fools of some of the department's most experienced men."

Inwardly I bridled a little. I'd done more than sink bull's-eyes in targets and chase down clues. I'd made a name for myself in helping mend fences between the police and the black community of my precinct, which to a last person had risen up to defend me in spite of my having killed one of their own. Me, a white woman, more or less. It had helped the jury dismiss the charge of murder the prosecutor had tried unsuccessfully to pin on me.

Gutierrez, leaning his aging bulk against his desk and staring at me across it as though looking right into my mind, then said with a strange kind of intensity, "But I want something else. Something more important than any of that. I want you to tell me something. And straight. No hedging. It won't be easy for you, but I need to know."

He paused, never taking his eyes from mine, and then said, "Just between you and me, okay? I want you to tell me exactly how you felt from the moment you walked into the bodega until you shot the bastard. You answered the call, you burst in the door, and he was standing at the counter pointing his gun at the proprietor, and you shouted 'Freeze' and 'Drop your gun,' if I read the report correctly. And then what? I want you to fill me in on every single second of it. Not what you did—I know all that—but how you *felt* when you did it. What was happening in your head?"

He waited. And in spite of myself it all came

back on me in a rush: the guy swinging his stolen police Glock around on me and spitting hate
and screaming "Mother-fuckah" and so quick that
before I could pull my trigger there was the blind-
ing flash of pain as the gun's barrel slashed like
lightning across my forehead with my own gun
wrenched away. My somehow getting a hand on
his gun, then—it all happened so fast—and my trying to bring him down by force, aware suddenly of
his huge size, he was twice as big as me, the horrible smell and heat of him and the hopelessness
of it, but to get him down anyway, somehow, my
thinking only how to do it and thinking insanely of
how I was going to manage all alone to get the cuffs
on him once he *was* down, my struggle to hold the
Glock away from me, the roar of the several shots
he pulled that went wild, and then another as I used
the kickback to finally twist the Glock around and
heard the next shot that took him to the floor with
me on top of him.

I slowly refocused on Gutierrez and took a deep
breath.

"Not what you *did,* Kasie, we know all that." He
repeated. "How you *felt.* Not before; not afterward.
During."

I fumbled a moment, trying to remember. And
then I did. I met his eyes and said, "I don't know.
It was like being stuck with any job that had to be
done and done right. It was like when I took an

exam at school, I didn't think about messing up. All I thought about was the business of doing it and doing it right. It was like that."

Even as I spoke, I felt a kind of light laughter surge out of me at a long forgotten memory. "Or," I said, "like the time one of Dad's cows went crazy dangerous, and he was away, and I had to get her down and was holding onto her head so Mom could get a twitch on her nose, and me twisting it around, like bulldogging a steer, and trying as hard as possible to get her off balance and over. I could only think, '*Do it*. Not that I couldn't. Just get her down, Kasie. I couldn't think of anything else."

I stopped, suddenly embarrassed at saying so much, and as though admitting to something indecent. Gutierrez leaned back and laughed. "Okay," he said. "You've just told me how you act under severe stress, which too many cops don't handle well. So here's the deal, and if you don't want to do it, just say so."

Once more I waited, wondering. Then he said, "You've heard of Connors Warriner, the former governor? Owns Delta Red."

I had. Who hadn't? The once governor had outlived multiple, corruption scandals. "Yes, sir."

"Do you know about Lonsdale Hall?"

I did. "Yes, sir. I've seen pictures of it." And I had. It was right out of *Gone with the Wind*, a classic brick plantation home, its front entrance graced with soaring white columns. It was on an island in the Bayou Teche near New Iberia southwest of Baton Rouge and probably the crown jewel of all the historic plantation houses that remained.

Gutierrez flipped open a file other than mine and, glancing down at it, said, "It's been in the Warriner family for the past six or more generations. Old Warriner himself lives there. He was long a key figure in state and national politics, as you must know, and when governor always managed to successfully escape corruption charges. Now he's out of it, in a wheelchair. Alzheimer's."

"Then there's his elderly spinster sister, Sarah, a Southern lady of the old school and said to be a narrow, bigoted tyrant. And there's Congressman Connors Warriner Junior, who has taken over Delta Red and is known to everyone as a coldly arrogant son-of-a-bitch, except for the fools who voted him in to office.

"Connors Junior has a second wife of three years, Charlotte. She's dominant in Louisiana society, and there's a slightly younger sister, Felicity, in her early forties. She's childlike, or simply 'off' somehow, and living in her own world. Finally there's a brother, Ashley, who is flauntingly gay and doesn't work, but we know nothing more about him than that he plays tennis all the time.

"Connors Junior's first wife died in a waterskiing accident three years ago, and another older brother,

Arthur, who was a severe asthmatic, died twenty-five years before that when somebody put hot pepper into his inhaler; they never discovered who. A disgruntled servant was the only suspect, and some said that he'd been done in by Connors Junior, who was next in line for the entire estate. Nobody could pin it on him, however, or on an accomplice, and his father managed to silence the press.

"There's a social secretary, also, a Miss Davies, and a woman named Fredericka Mayworth, the family business manager. She's rumored to be the one making a deal with Reb Bannerman of B&R foods to take over Delta, but that's only rumor. The Warriners used to produce all the secret ingredients that went into the famous Delta Red hot sauce on some of the thousand acres of land the house is on, but all that agriculture, along with processing and bottling up the sauce, is now done in Tennessee."

Gutierrez closed the file and said, "How would you like to spend a week there as a photojournalist for *Great American Families* magazine? When I simply stared, my mouth slightly open in surprise and wondering what was coming next, he explained. "You'd be deputized by me as an FBI agent but given a Baton Rouge police ID and go undercover on special short assignment, probably lasting not longer than ten days and with photojournalism your cover. We have reason to believe that Connors Junior is up to no good, specifically that he might be a pedophile with connections to a large ring. He's our prime suspect and the reason for all of this. We've decided to try a plant whose job would be to closely observe him and maybe pick up something definite. Would that fit into your current schedule?"

It was the last thing I'd ever expected, and it caught me completely off guard. I finally found my voice. "Well, I guess maybe, but why me?"

Gutierrez broke into a fatherly kind of smile. He said, "Because you answer all the job requirements, and at the same time look so surprisingly innocent that nobody would ever take you for the great cop you were, let alone an undercover agent working with the feds."

I silently counted to ten, maybe more, making him wait. And finally put into words something I always tried to avoid, tried not even to think of anymore. I said, "A good cop, sure. But what about all the uproar?"

"What about it? I'm waiving all of it."

That threw me a bit. He had clearly sifted through every miserable inch of my whole sordid New Orleans story, and was ignoring it. It made me want to do right by him. I said, "Anything particular I'd be looking for?" And finally relaxed all the way.

"Anything and everything," he said, and told me about the phrase "girls to be" injected oddly into financial talk about a takeover and possibly hinting pedophilia. "It could be just a planned night out at a brothel," he said, "or it could possibly be worse. I stress *possibly.* But Washington wants to see if it ties into the international hookup they're after in Malaysia and Thailand. If it does, it could make planting someone among them precarious. I want to be clear about that."

I suddenly had difficulty listening. More came back on me again, this time something I'd once seen when a cop. They'd found a dead child in a sewage canal, a little girl with her hands and feet tied with rusty wire. She's been beaten and tortured and the pathologist said repeatedly raped but was still alive when thrown into the canal to drown. Various suspected serial killers and pedophiles had been rounded up and questioned but they'd all had iron-clad alibis.

So before Gutierrez could speak again, I knew I'd take the job.

"My cover," I said. "I mean, okay, The *Great American Families* rag. Who are they? And are they in on this?"

"All the way. They're a glossy prestigious national with a surprisingly high subscription rate with people who go for society stuff. Both the publisher and the senior editor were briefed extensively last week and are fully cooperative. They don't know what we are investigating, only that we are. The editor contacted the Warriner family to explain they wanted to do an article on them and Lonsdale Hall, and asked if they could put one of their top reporters up for ten days or so, and got their agreement." He smiled. "People love to be written about; I don't care who they are. As long as they don't know there's an ulterior motive behind it."

He pulled two glossy copies of *Great American Families* from his desk drawer and pushed them across the desk at me. "First day of homework," he said. "Get busy."

FIVE

When I actually saw Lonsdale Hall, it was everything it appeared to be in all the pictures I'd studied. It took my breath away. Okay for the past, but were there actually people who lived that way today? Rising early, I'd packed up things for a week's stay, including special equipment provided by Gutierrez. I'd called in advance and was due first thing in the morning, and after I'd left the main highway in my old Toyota, had traveled a half mile on a branch road before I reached the arched stone bridge that spanned the narrow Bayou Teche and connected the island to the mainland.

Crossing the bridge over the quiet sluggish water, I pulled up to collect myself just short of a long avenue of magnificent southern live oaks, whose wide spreading branches, arched over from each side, formed an arbor ceiling above the white gravel driveway leading to the great old house.

A score of images raced through my mind: the figures of slaves at work like dark shadows, booted, overseeing gentry on horseback, whips in hand, women in flowered hats and flowing skirts playing croquet on the carefully tended lawn enclosed by the driveway, which ended in a circle before the wide stone steps up to magnificent double doors. Opened, they revealed the coolness of the mansion's spacious front hall, from where a sweeping curved stairway led to the floor above.

There'd been a life here that was no longer. There'd been Southern belles flirting and weddings and funerals and childbirth and children's laughter and young men in the gray uniforms of the Confederacy going off to war and their deaths. There'd been a gentle aristocratic and easy way of life never repeated.

But evil has many forms and takes on many disguises, and all the while there'd been nearly universal oblivion to the tragedy that it all existed on the backs of black families ripped asunder and with no rights except to belong to a "master"—tortured souls from far-distant Africa torn from their homes and transported in chains, bodies crushed against bodies in fetid, rat-infested, windowless slave ships, all personal identity lost, while there'd been outraged hostility by their owners toward anyone who dared to raise a hand in their defense.

Taking a moment longer, I reviewed some of my two weeks' intensive preparation for what I was about to do. I mentally refamiliarized every corner of the house, then checked off names: Old Connors Warriner Senior, Aunt Sarah, old Warriner's spinster sister, Connors Junior, the congressman, sister Felicity, brother Ashley, and a Miss Davies, the secretary, and Fredericka Mayworth, the business manager.

Finally there was one whom Gutierrez had missed but whom I had spotted doing my research and thought might turn out to be important, though how and why I had no idea. It was only a far-out hunch. This was Missy, an elderly black woman who had been nurse to all the Warriner children and still helped out with old Warriner Senior and who, as though segregation still existed, was housed with eight other servants—Erik, a butler, along with four housemaids, a cook, a scullery maid, and a janitor—in a shabby unseen brick building hidden at the back of Lonsdale Hall with all its grandeur and surrounded by a tight concealing hedge of arborvitae.

In my own research, I'd also learned about Miss Davies from an Internet blog sponsored by a black activist newsletter. She was unpleasantly described as an ever-silent, figureless, primly proper, late-middle-aged, self-righteous spinster who, I learned, garnished a disapproving and authoritarian personality with a pince-nez on a cord looped around a narrow area between her head and shoulders which seemed to substitute for a neck. She came promptly every day at ten in an anonymous two door Chevrolet sedan—from where, it was never explained—and apparently departed always promptly at four for a Second Church of Christ, Scientist, of which she was a member, at nearby New Iberia, where she was in charge of distributing Bibles and various religious tracts.

Finally, there were two other nonfamily people. The first was Fredericka Mayworth, known as Freddie, the family business and financial affairs manager. Pictures had shown her to be a good-looking, thoroughly modern woman, not yet fifty, who dressed stylishly, wore expensive costume jewelry, and had an athletic build. She owned a luxury apartment in a Baton Rouge condo overlooking the Mississippi but apparently preferred to stay much of the time at Lonsdale Hall, where her respected and oft authoritative presence made her a virtual member of the family.

The second, who had no connection with the family, was Clarence Hart-Bromley. The once scion of a prominent English family (his father was Lord Henry Hart-Bromley, OBE), he had gone bad while with the British Foreign Service in Singapore. Become a heavy drinker and hedonist, he was one of those decadent "old boys" portrayed in old movies as near native fixtures in some far-flung exotic cities of the former empire and was suspected of sex-trafficking by Interpol. I was particularly ordered to keep a weather eye opened for any mention or sign of him while at the Hall. "He's a bad one," Gutierrez had told me.

I glanced at my photo equipment on the seat next to me, the Canon Mark 3 along with its separate telephoto and wide-angle lenses that had been provided for me by the *Great American Families* magazine. Besides glamor shots of Lonsdale Hall and its surroundings, I was to take mug shots of everyone for the FBI as well as casuals, along with gathering their fingerprints, neither of which presented difficulty.

But the pictures wouldn't be with the Canon. The guys in the FBI tech lab had rigged it as a sensitive and silent sound recorder. Whatever pictures I took, and they would be numerous, would surreptitiously be taken with either my iPhone or iPad while seeming to use the Canon.

More difficult than any pictures would be getting into both private and business correspondence and, as much as possible, into laptops and PCs, if any, of which the FBI had no record. Gutierrez had also counseled me to be constantly on the alert for any talk or word I might overhear that could lead to evidence, and I'd been provided for those times, when I wasn't carrying the Canon, with a second tiny microrecorder disguised as a wristwatch.

"Try as much as possible, Kasie," Gutierrez counseled, "to fit into the family, gain the personal confidence of each one. You should always be of two minds. One half of you should feel completely innocent; you are there only as a photojournalist to do an article on the great house and the family who occupies it. The other half is to spy on them, to get into whatever there might be in their private lives that could incriminate. You've got the emergency code?"

"Yes, sir."

"If you can't reach me on normal channels, don't hesitate to use the red-alert if we actually are onto something hooked into, say, the Malaysians or the Thais, and they should find out that we are. That crowd doesn't kid around."

The red-alert he referred to was a tiny chip he'd ordered inserted under the skin of my right hip, revealed at the moment only by a Band-Aid. I had only to press it three times consecutively.

"Yes, sir," I'd said. "I understand that."

I closed my eyes and leaned back in my seat, wondering briefly, as I had for days, what it was going to be like, belonging for a week at least to the famous Warriner family, which might harbor in its midst a sick and even dangerous pedophile. I'd had more than one moment when I'd wondered if I was actually up to the job. How was I going to fit in with the ex-governors and society dowagers who apparently were often visitors? I'd been brought up mostly innocent of what had to be the totally different lifestyle of the moneyed class, to say nothing of their attitudes. Secretly, I blessed my mother, who had insisted on good manners at all times. At least I had that as comfort, and with it the further thought that if Gutierrez considered me good enough for the job, that I probably was; he was no fool. Nor was the big boss, Tom Whitman, who had spent thirty minutes with me over coffee not just chatting but sizing me up, I knew, the day after Gutierrez had asked me to take on the job.

Realizing now that I'd waited so long parked there just off the bridge and at the foot of the driveway that I could have aroused suspicion of some sort, I put the old Toyota in Drive, and not without a certain reluctance and anxiety, started up the long avenue under the trees, the car's tires crunching loudly on the carefully raked white gravel. I was on my own, and the sheer isolation of myself was frightening.

I wasn't even Kasie any longer. Gutierrez had seen to that—at least not where the Warriners were concerned. When I'd taken on the job, I'd been instructed to mentally erase any of my real background. Revelation of where I actually came from and who my family actually was would more than likely have had one of the Warriners on the phone before sundown to Arkansas, where my parents might innocently give away the real me. Therefore, Gutierrez had created a fictional past for me and arranged verification of it with the editor of *Great American Families.* "I'm giving you one," he'd said, "that they can never trace you to, if even innocently they should try."

So now I was Joanne Henley, the daughter of a leading Baltimore socialite who was on the board of Johns Hopkins University. I had gone to a privileged boarding school in New England and my coming-out debut had been one of the seasons most important. I had a good memory, and after an evening of using it on a list of Baltimore socialites, could glibly rattle off a dozen names.

"You're Joanne, and don't you forget it," I told myself fiercely as I reached the end of the arbor of trees and parked half way round the driveway's circles before the house. "Not for one instant."

SIX

Felicity had set herself and her paint things, an easel mounted by a large pad of expensive watercolor paper and a table for a small bowl of water, her paints and brushes by a vase of cut flowers in the shade of a big lilac bush, one of a hedge-like row of them off one end of Lonsdale Hall that separated the house and the area before it from formal gardens beyond which, in miniature, were patterned after those at Versailles.

It was two days after my arrival, and as I watched from the driveway where I was photographing the historic plantation house, or seeming to with my faked Canon mounted on a tripod, I saw her making sure the hairs on the paint brush were pressed into a fine point by wetting and twisting them slightly. Then, bending close to the easel, she began very carefully to write her name in slender little letters at the bottom of the finished watercolor she'd painted of the vase of flowers.

She had written Felicity and had only just finished with the first *r* in Warriner when her brother Ashley suddenly came tripping out of the house and headed for an expensive convertible parked by the driveway circle, its driver, a young man with flamboyant dyed-blond hair, and I swear wearing makeup, clearly waiting for him. When Ashley spotted Felicity, he waved at the waiting driver then veered toward his sister, whose concentration he abruptly shattered in a loud voice that was pitched oddly upward into a near twitter.

"Why are you writing your name, Felicity? Do you think anyone would ever care who painted those silly flowers?"

Felicity, the second *r* in Warriner yet to be started, didn't reply, and I, only yards away, didn't have to think much to know why. Ever since I'd arrived at Lonsdale Hall, Ashley had never stopped making fun of her painting. And it wasn't just Ashley; it was everyone, especially Charlotte, who had a special way of sneering at it. Charlotte would say, "I see, Felicity. How delightful. Another masterpiece. Are those flowers you painted?" As if she couldn't see that they were indeed flowers, or at least meant to be, and to Felicity perhaps perfectly rendered.

Ashley waited for a reply. He was wearing tennis shoes and shorts that made his thin legs look even thinner along with a white Lacoste tennis shirt that he thought hid the shallow thinness of his chest, and that meant that instead of tennis on the Lonsdale courts as usual, he was going to watch a match at a country club with the tennis pro who came twice a week from Baton Rouge to give him lessons. When Felicity didn't answer, he said with an unpleasant tone of spite, "Cat got your tongue?" And when she still didn't respond, "Suit yourself, then," and he simpered away, leaving her to be alone again.

I didn't think Felicity minded being alone. She almost always was. It was better for her than having to be with anyone and talk and be pulled away from her thoughts, which I was told were mostly about the people in the storybooks that Missy still haltingly read to her, along with the stories Missy told her sometimes, when no one was around, about her own black people. Missy, I'd already observed, would sneak to Felicity's bedroom at bedtime, and when she was in bed, hold her hand and whisper so as not to be caught and lectured by Charlotte, or worse, by Aunt Sarah, who often told the old lady to "Stop talking nonsense to Felicity. She doesn't understand a word you're saying anyway."

Apparently there'd been brain damage of some

sort at birth. There was a prettiness about her, however, that shone through her almost childish face, and a fastidiousness about her person that denied the dowdiness of her clothes that would have been more suitable on a sixty-year-old. She was quite capable of looking after herself, dressing and undressing, bathing and hygiene, and although on the surface she seemed perfectly normal, she mostly lived in some kind of fantasy world of her own, endlessly painting vases of flowers in the house or individual groups of flowers out in the formal gardens.

Old Missy appeared to be her only true friend. Everyone else was "them," especially Aunt Sarah. She was the first "them." Connors Junior was the second. Or maybe it was Charlotte. With Aunt Sarah it was, "Do try to be like the rest of us, Felicity. The Warriners have standards. And try to remember that the servants must always be kept in their place so they don't get ideas."

With Connors Junior it was, "For heaven's sake, Aunt Sarah, do we have to have her here? Can't she be put in a home with her own kind?" I knew Felicity hated Connors Junior, who was always talking *about* her, not *to* her even when standing right next to her or at the table when they ate dinner.

The congressman, my prime suspect, didn't talk much to anyone else either. He just ordered everyone about, except for Charlotte and Fredericka

Mayworth, with whom he was constantly meeting in the room upstairs that had been turned into an office with a printer and copy machine and a desk and some files. The place was strictly off-limits to Felicity, just like Charlotte's office, guarded by Miss Davies, who sat at a desk in an anteroom and either typed endlessly away at her computer or talked to someone on the telephone.

The moment Ashley was driven away, I abandoned my Canon on its tripod and walked over to Felicity and said softly so as not to startled her, "Hi, Felicity."

It was just as Felicity got to the final letter in Warriner, and regardless of my good intention she *was* startled. When she turned to see who it was and found out it was just the lady who had come to stay and take pictures for some magazine smiling down at her, she almost became a different person.

"Hi," she said.

She had taken a shine to me from the moment I'd arrived. She couldn't ever remember my name and just called me "Lady" or "the lady" to others, and she told old Missy that she thought I was ever so nice and never sneered at her watercolors and that I talked to her and right in front of everybody, too. It hadn't escaped me that I seemed the only one who ever spoke to her other than Missy, and that when I did, Charlotte always looked annoyed. On my first day at breakfast, when all I said was something like, "Good morning, Felicity. Did you sleep well?" Or, "What are you painting today?" she sniffed disapproval, while her husband lowered his newspaper and muttered something about "wasting your time."

When Felicity smiled back up at me from before her easel, it struck me, as always, that her simplicity was so odd in a grown-up woman my own age or slightly older. I put a hand on her shoulder and bent to inspect the confusion of colors that Felicity said were the flowers she had painted. They were, as all the flowers she painted so endlessly every day, impossible to recognize as such. What I saw on the easel was a jumble of colors, as though someone had simply brushed paint willy-nilly and in every direction on the paper.

I tried to sound sincere, and it wasn't really hard to. The poor woman deserved caring more than honesty. "Oh, Felicity, that's just lovely."

"Do you really like it?"

"I most certainly do. You're ever such a good artist." And thought, *Such a lost soul.*

Flattering Felicity's so-called watercolor brought home to me almost more than anything the charade I was acting. From the moment I'd started up the long arbored-over driveway to Lonsdale Hall,

I'd been forcibly aware that my acting a part had finally begun. This wasn't the endless briefings and preparatory studying I'd done on every single one of the Warriners, the hours I'd spent on the phone with the editor of *Great American Families* so that I'd be prepared to answer any questions about the magazine. This was *it*.

Aware as I drove and the beautiful old antebellum mansion got closer and closer that there was no pulling back, I'd been struck with a nervousness I'd almost never experienced, not even during my worst moments as a police officer. Would I be able to pull off this assignment, or would I somehow, somewhere, at some time make some sort of serious mistake and be exposed?

Getting evidence wasn't going to be easy. I could hardly prowl around the house at night, go into people's rooms when they were asleep, or even into office space while never knowing if someone would unexpectedly awaken and wonder why I was still up. And in the day, there would always be people around most of the time.

Visions raced in my head of a disappointed Jermyn Gutierrez, faced with possible official backlash but hiding his annoyance and pretending my failure was all right; he'd hardly dared expect success. And with all that a fear that if I didn't play my cards right and be absolutely convincing as a photojournalist, I might suddenly find myself in serious danger if indeed Connors Junior was involved with a criminal ring.

The first moments on the job were the worst, when I was greeted at the door of Lonsdale Hall by the trim and attractive Warriner family business manager, whose very appearance, in a tailored designer suit, spelled money and set her apart from all the rest. "Miss Henley, welcome to Lonsdale Hall. I'm Frederica Mayworth, and please just call me Freddie. Everyone else does."

"Am I too early?" I was afraid that I probably was.

"No. Not at all. The family never breakfasts until nearly nine, and they've just finished and are all spread around the living room at the moment, reading the newspaper or whatever, and I know dying to meet you. But let's get you settled first."

I was promptly taken upstairs to a rather distant guest room to leave my things, and the opulence of what I saw on the way took my breath away. From the front hall, from which I could see, through wide double doors on opposite sides of it, both the living room and the dining room, and then, in rooms we passed on the way to mine, the entire interior, represented a world that hadn't changed since 1850 and was vividly expressed everywhere by priceless Federalist antiques.

From canopied four-poster beds, marble-topped dressers, dressing tables, writing desks and highboys, from mahogany secretaries to dazzling crystal chandeliers and candelabras, from heavily gilded frames enclosing the portraits of every War-riner patriarch down through the years along with similarly framed portraits of their ladies, noth-ing had changed, Freddie said, as she pointed out everything's importance. Everything was exactly as it was since the first day of the beautiful plantation home's occupancy by the Warriner family.

Even though I had endlessly studied pictures of all of it, seeing it for real was staggering. Where had all this priceless furniture, bric-a-brac, drapery, and incredible picture frames come from? I knew a little about antiques, as my mother had always been interested in the different kinds over the dif-ferent ages and in different countries, so that I knew much of the stuff had been imported from Europe and not native to America. It had all been carefully packed and crated and shipped across the Atlantic to be daily dusted and polished and kept in immac-ulate condition by household slaves, whose similar trip across the ocean had been appallingly different.

I quickly settled, and Freddie took me back down-stairs, where I was ushered to the living room and found the family more or less awaiting me like a jury assembled for a trial and getting ready to judge.

"Here she is, everyone," Freddie said cheerfully.

"Joanne Henley. We've all been so eagerly waiting for you, Miss Henley."

My "Welcome to Lonsdale Hall" greeting by Charlotte, mistress of the house and Connors Junior's second wife of three years, seemed not so much an effort as it was perfunctory. She rose from one of several uncomfortable-looking Federalist sofas some distance from her congressman husband, who was sprawled on a recamier sofa.

She was a big, heavily bosomed woman in her fifties whose large lips were emphasized by too much lipstick and whose prominent, almost protruding upper teeth dominated a slightly receding chin. Her immaculately coiffed blond hair, which she wore fairly short and swept back, was tinted bluish to disguise slowly invading gray. I was surprised at her clothes. She had on what I thought an outrageously bad-taste floral-print dress that matched somehow an aura about her of total social snobbery. She looked older than her husband and reminded me of a schoolteacher I'd had who always belabored us with wretchedly bad early morning breath. While I wondered at the social power she apparently yielded, I also wondered why Connors Junior, or anyone else, for that matter, would have ever wanted to marry her.

With my presence announced, Freddie turned to a brittle, overly made-up antiquity stationed on the embroidered cushions of what was inappropriately a love seat. "Aunt Sarah, this is Miss Henley, who *Great American Families* has sent down to do an article about us."

And I found myself examined by a look that said, "Don't you dare challenge me," which was etched in every one of the many old-age lines seaming an overly powdered imperious face and belonged, as did the rest of Aunt Sarah's appearance, to long bygone years. She sat rigidly erect, her withered neck encircled by a tight velvet choker ribbon that was nearly lost beneath folds of sagging jowls. Coils of amethyst and tourmaline beads fell from around it down over the lacy sunken bosom of a dress that had been in style among the Edwardians. Like a frozen statue, her body language alone expressed disapproval of such an intrusion by a stranger, and when she spoke a required courtesy welcome, her voice reminded me of an old-fashioned porcelain miniature.

"You must be very tired from your voyage, Miss Henley. Such a very long way."

Voyage? Long way? Oh, of course, she'd picked up on *Great American Families* being published in Baltimore, and had decided I'd driven from there. I replied that I'd stopped on the way and felt thoroughly rested. Her next remark was even more unexpected and actually a question, as though Baltimore was a small village where everyone knew everyone else. "I'm sure you must know my dear friend Eleanor Wainwright."

My head spun. Somehow I remembered the name from among the socialites I'd been rehearsed to say I knew so as to lend authenticity in my coming from there. I said as blandly as I could, "I haven't seen her, Miss Warriner, since my coming-out ball. She was on the committee. But I believe she's well."

She sniffed contentedly. "She was originally from here and shared my coming-out with me, but then most unfortunately she married a Baltimore person."

And said no more. Meanwhile, I caught a quick glimpse of Charlotte's expression. It was one of slightly startled surprise. She hadn't expected me to be so classy.

Connors Junior was a different question entirely. His father being nearly superfluous to my story, I shall from this point on drop the junior and refer to him simply as Connors. It was instantly quite clear that my being there and the article in *Great American Families* was of no interest whatsoever to him. That was Charlotte's department. Slouched on the recamier, his legs widespread, almost obscenely, he lowered a newspaper to rise, as expected of him, and all the polished politician, extending a chubby manicured hand and with welcoming words he must have used on a thousand constituents when they came to his office or whom he greeted on the hustings.

I instantly reminded myself that this was a man suspected of a dangerous and sick sexual proclivity and the reason why I was there. He set my teeth on edge. I'd seen pictures, of course, but they all had minimized his soft, pale-white overweight, the pudginess of his short fingers, so at odds with his considerable height—I guessed six foot four. Indeed, pudgy might have described all of him, from his rapidly balding head with its wispy remnants of thin pale-blond hair to his rather small feet that were clad in extremely expensive tasseled moccasins and which, given his softly unmuscular belly that folded obtrusively over his belt, must have been hard for him to see. He had slightly bulbous and lusterless eyes and a face surrounding both that was equally void of any expression. He was a human version of a frog, and I had a quick vision of him as a little boy pulling the wings off flies. Just the way I couldn't imagine anyone wanting to marry Charlotte, I found it beyond me that anyone would ever want to vote for him.

Ashley, whom I hadn't first seen, suddenly appeared. He'd been half hidden, seated on an ottoman in a far corner like a troll, and now stood up, a physical reed of simpering falseness and so different in appearance from his congressman brother, as he stood fidgeting nervously, that he evoked instant mistrust in me. With his slightly tittering welcome that was laced with burst of laughter (about what?), he reminded me of certain weasel-like informers I'd known as a cop, and an inner voice warned, *Watch out for this one. He's without principles, and I bet is the worst kind of sickly gossip.*

Felicity was there, of course, looking lost and silent, her hands folded in her lap and her eyes downcast, and to me, oddly enough, somehow the only one who seemed aristocratic and to belong there.

To say the least, the whole family were something of a surprise. I don't know now what I expected, perhaps a more patriarchal, even statesman-like sort of people, perhaps dignified Old South patricians, the last gentry of a once grand aristocracy with genteel manners and dress—in effect, people whom I would see as virtually matching in style the elegance of their home.

They seemed, however, quite ordinary and like people I could meet anywhere, and I was immediately struck that Freddie stood out in comparison as the one among them who was fashionably smart and part of a whole new flow and style of life that had seized the world. Although well-mannered, as we conversed and made small talk for a few minutes, and with Charlotte expressing her pleasure at the forthcoming article about them in *Great American Families,* I sensed at once that the Warriners were people whose manners were for the most part superficial, and found myself at that early point in our acquaintance unable to judge what each one of them was really like. I also found myself wishing I could have met them one by one rather than in a group and introduced to them almost as though I were a gawking tourist on vacation tour of the stately plantation home with the good luck to meet the famous owners.

None of that first impression was made any better with the appearance of Connors Warriner Senior. The former governor was wheeled in by Erik, the giant black butler. A large blob of a man with a balding head and an aging face that was utterly vacant of any expression that showed he was aware of his whereabouts, he was strapped into his chair and slumped down as though his body was already as far gone as his mind. It was hard to imagine that what I saw had once been a famous and powerfully corrupt politician who had bought and sold political offices as though a retail merchant. The family said nothing, and in an awkward silence it was left for Erik to politely turn to me and say, "Colonel Warriner, ma'am."

The senior Warriner's appearance, once he was announced, provoked a remark by Charlotte that expressed false embarrassment at his presence along with her hope that "Miss Henley would avoid dwelling on his unfortunate condition when writing up her article."

Not a problem, I thought. His presence aroused

in me an immediate desire to flee his presence as soon as possible. He brought *Sic semper tyrannis* to mind, and after a few more minutes of small talk, I managed to extricate myself from any further awkwardness by stating as cheerfully as I could that I had best get to work; there was so much to do to justify my being there and grant the family the honor they deserved.

Glancing back as I departed, I saw them still widely spread about the room like so many cardboard cutouts, just as they had been when I'd entered. Aunt Sarah had picked up some knitting from the dark surface of a Sicilian-marble side table, Connors had returned to his newspaper, Felicity hadn't moved and still stared at her lap, twisting her hands together, and Ashley had disappeared. Only Charlotte continued to fix eyes on me as I left with Freddie. And I thought that there had to be a whole lot more about the Warriner family that Jermyn Gutierrez hadn't briefed me on.

SEVEN

That first day I was seated for luncheon with all of the family at the long dining room table, its highly-polished mahogany surface formally set with Wedgewood china, Baccarat crystal glasses, and the finest sterling silverware. I had regained command of my senses. I'd d even begun to think of myself as Joanne Henley. I was authority, I reminded myself. I wasn't being investigated, *they* were. And one of them was perhaps seriously guilty of criminal activity.

All my powers of investigating that had served me so well in the detective division of the New Orleans Police took over. I stopped thinking about myself or to be blinded by surroundings so utterly new to me and thought only about *them,* the famed Warriner family. Once I'd been with them a while, I got over my disappointment at their seeming relatively ordinary, and simply accepted each one on his or her own terms, which I began to discover bit by bit, so that instead of Warriners they became individuals whose characters were composed on many levels.

I knew before I'd even started the drive out their way from the Bureau's Baton Rouge headquarters that I'd need to present myself as something a little more than a photojournalist if I was ever going to gain the confidence of any one of them, or if not confidence, then at least lessen the sort or silent, oddly defensive barrier I suspected they might put up between us, which is true of so many being photographed or interviewed. So I reluctantly allowed them to drag my Baltimore social background out of me and to act as though I'd always belonged in the rarified bubble in which they had cocooned themselves. Almost to my surprise, I found myself completely at ease in answering their formally awkward questions about the magazine article I was preparing as well as in asking them questions of my own.

At the same time, I instinctively observed— although masked by the formality of their manners, which I sensed to be mostly false—that there seemed a strain among them. Not because of my presence but between themselves. There seemed a carefully covered-over animosity that festered, each family member on edge with every one of the others. Only an always silent Felicity seemed free of it.

They don't at all love each other, I suddenly realized, *let alone even like one another very much.* A second thought was that *They're hiding something shared.* And I felt a chill run through my body, the kind I'd had as a cop when something didn't seem right on a seemingly quiet street when I was a rookie and on night patrol. Could they somehow be disguising as much evil as their ancestors had two centuries before them?

It wasn't old Warriner's Alzheimer's, I knew. With none of the family speaking of him or even to him, he sat at the head of the table, a wasted mound of decaying flesh without a mind, a sadly wilted cauliflower. Belying his having once been a feared and unforgiving figure, his eyes were glazed and looked at nothing as, ever silent, he was spoon-fed by Erik, whose obsequiousness in such a big and powerful man in the modern world I thought totally odd.

Once they had become relatively used to me, I found myself being almost taken for granted, as though I'd always been there. Beneath polite remarks and questions about the article, there was none of the interest and excitement I'd expected in their being intimately viewed by a reporter for a national magazine, nor the opposite—a sort of discomfort that I'd thought would also be natural in people who would feel their private life "exposed," even though clearly welcoming it.

After lunch the old man was wheeled away to the open lift that had been installed to take him up and down. His once study had for a while been used by his son as an office at home but now, unused for several years, was firmly closed. The very large living room, the library, the dining room, and kitchen occupied the rest of the ground floor.

As I left the dining room myself, Freddie said, "Come join me, Joanne. I've got some background material for you that might be of help," and I went upstairs with her to the immaculate and very modern office that had been converted from a once small sitting room. When she'd gone to her desk and had indicated a comfortable chair for me, she'd wasted little time in giving me a general travel agent's picture of Lonsdale Hall and its residents. "You haven't seen the property yet. I'll delegate Ashley to show it to you tomorrow, although, other than the gardens, there isn't much to see. As Delta Red's sales soared and more and more ingredients were needed, old Warriner had the whole farming operation moved north to land he owned in Tennessee. All that's left to show that the ingredients for the sauce were once grown here are two huge fields beyond the gardens to the north, or 'up bayou' as we say, while there are several more fields, now gone to brush beyond the house in the other direction."

"And now Delta Red's for sale?" It was a shot in the dark I thought worth trying.

Freddie's reaction was immediate. "For sale? Good heavens, whoever told you that?"

"One of my colleagues, when he learned I was coming here. If it's just rumor, journalists pick up all sorts of things."

"Well, rumor is exactly what it is, nothing more," Freddie said firmly. "The Warriners aren't about to sell any part of Delta Red."

The moment she said it, I felt a wave of disillusion. "Not selling Delta Red" caught me completely by surprise. Why on earth was she denying it, and in a way that said, "Don't challenge what I say," and which almost seemed a warning? *But it's a fact, why lie about it,* I said to myself. It seemed completely out of character with Fredericka's personality and demeanor, and I realized that its mere blatancy indicated I might expect more of the same from her.

I decided any further questions from me on Delta Red right then would be overplaying my hand, so I said, "We won't write about it, of course, or anything else without your approval. You will see all copy before it goes to the printers. That will be true, also, for the death of Connors's first wife, which must have been quite a shock for everyone here."

The business manager's expression instantly

grew somber. "You know about that, I see. Of course, you would have had to do some research on us here before you came." And then, "Joanne, shock is putting it mildly. It created sheer hell for weeks. I suppose because we're such a famous family that the police for some idiotic reason—perhaps just a chance to bask in publicity for themselves—decided the death perhaps wasn't an accident, and we had them all over the place for days. It was ridiculous and completely unwarranted. As if Connors's grief and everyone else's wasn't enough for us to handle."

"I take it Candice was very well liked, then."

"Not liked, *loved*. She was the most wonderful free spirit you could ever imagine. And so full of life. It's still impossible to realize that she is no more."

"And yet," I ventured, "Connors married fairly soon afterward, didn't he?"

"Eighteen months."

"Had he known Charlotte before the accident?"

"I believe they probably had met a few times. They travel the same social circles. Charlotte was a widow, and Connors, like so many men who were very happily married, dove right back into it."

Again surprised, I thought, *Chalk up lie number two*. Preparing for the job, I'd picked up that Connors's marriage to Candice was dramatically tempestuous and unhappy. "And what about Ashley?" I asked, getting away quickly from Connors and

Charlotte. "Any possibility there?"

Freddie smiled, a little maliciously, I thought. "If any guy will have him. At the moment, he's working on the tennis pro, name of Dennis—"Dennis the Tennis," we call him. Or Dennis is working on him, but I doubt anything materializes there." She paused, and her expression grew somber again. "And then of course there's Felicity, poor child."

"What happened there?"

"Nobody quite knows, Joanne. Her mother had a very difficult birth, and one doctor said the baby was deprived of oxygen for too long. Felicity's quite capable of keeping more or less to household schedule and obeying some basic household rules. It's just that she lives in a different world from the rest of us. Missy looks after her, mostly. Missy's the little black woman whom you'd take to be a hundred and probably is. She came here as a child and was nanny to all four children when they were little. Now she helps with the old man."

I glanced down at my laptop as though to check on a person, although it was hardly necessary. I had studied up on nearly everyone in the family for the past three generations and probably, I thought, knew more about any of them, including Missy, than Freddie did.

"Old Warriner's wife and their mother, what happened to her? I think I was told her name was Celine."

"Celine, yes. She died almost exactly thirty years ago. Pneumonia. Old Connors was a widower for a long time. She was before my day, obviously, but she was a Creole and reputedly a fireball."

"What's a Creole?" I know the answer but wanted to hear it from her.

"Native born and descended from one of the original French or Spanish families. And probably having some mixed blood."

There was a faint touch of disdain in her tone. Creoles were often of mixed African or even Native America blood. *Like me,* I thought. I said aloud, "What does the future look like for Warriner Senior? He seems pretty much out of it."

"The old man? Alzheimer's, and he's been out of it for some time now. His son and I both have power of attorney. Connors does nearly all of Delta Red, and I mind the family business, their investment portfolio, various trusts, and that sort of thing."

Lie three, I thought, and, *If anyone is managing Delta Red, it's you, since you seem to be carrying on all the negotiations with Reb Bannerman.* I pushed my chair back and rose, wondering why all three lies. What was she covering? I said, "But I'm taking up far too much of your time, Freddie. Don't worry about me further. I've a pile of photographing to do, and I'll want to talk to Charlotte, Connors, and Ashley individually, when they can find a moment for me. We'll need quotes from all three."

Freddie also rose and with a warm smile came from behind her desk and extended a hand. "I'll leave you to it, then, Joanne. The place is yours. Anything I can do to help you, just shout, okay?"

I felt a slight inner tremor. I still wasn't completely used to being called Joanne, or Miss Henley, which the overly formal Charlotte insisted on, and I dreaded a slip up—perhaps forgetting who I now was and not answering to either Joanne or Henley when spoken to. I reminded myself once again to be careful and to always think my new identity and never forget.

Leaving Freddie, I realized the one thing I didn't have to fake was photography, and deciding to waste no time getting at it, I went to collect the photographic equipment I would pretend to use.

EIGHT

I didn't like the thought of doing interviews. They seemed a distraction from what I was there for and a waste of time. But they were my cover, an appearance of doing a bona fide article for *Great American Families* that *had* to be kept up, and so I was stuck with them.

My first one was long after lunch on my second day and with Aunt Sarah, who condescended to speak to me in the sitting room of her suite upstairs. She had arisen from her daily afternoon nap and was seated in an expansive white wicker chair softened with several deep cushions. Her gray head was adorned with a lace cap and bent over a frame of petit point.

Not offering me a seat, the imperious old lady spoke to me in the tone of an ageing matriarch who sees herself as the all-important guardian of the family morals and social standing, and her first words quite caught me by surprise. Without looking up, she said," Who was your mother?"

The sheer unpleasant abruptness of her question startled me as much as, coming out of the blue, the very nature of the question itself. Who was my mother? What on earth? My coming from Baltimore and my social standing there had been thoroughly exposed. Could the old woman possibly have forgotten so soon? The memories of the aged were often fragile.

Or was there more? If she indeed had not forgotten, was I possibly being tested as to identity, and Aunt Sarah perhaps being chosen to give the question of my social standing an appearance of innocence? It was chilling to think that there might be suspicion of me. Had I slipped up somewhere already?

Answer, Kasie, I said to myself, *whatever her reasons, or the reasons of others,* so I said to her, and as candidly as I could, "I'm from Baltimore, Miss Warriner, remember?" and repeated my lunchtime revelation that my mom was a Harkness from the old New England family, and my father, when alive, had been on the board of Johns Hopkins.

Only partially mollified, Aunt Sarah favored

me with a dry cough. "Half a Yankee Harkness, are you? Why are you, then, working in such a lowly position?"

And I suddenly realized that before Aunt Sarah answered a single question, she wanted to reassure herself that she was speaking to someone of her own class. Inwardly laughing at my fears, I cautioned myself yet again against my constant fear of slipping up somehow and being revealed, and said, "It's just my first step in learning the magazine business, Miss Warriner. I'm to take over a cousin's firm later on. He publishes upmarket magazines like *Yachting America* and *Country Estates.*

Another deathly silence. Downcast gray eyes, above thin disapproving lips withered with age, studied the petit point. Until apparently reassured she wasn't about to reveal family information to an inferior working-class person, the old woman said in a less imperious tone, "You have correctly addressed yourself to the right person in seeking any family information. Most unfortunately, the younger generation today are hopelessly ignorant of their forebears' distinguished history, let alone of their own superior position because of it."

Tired of standing and seeing a stool, I took a chance and pulled it up to sit opposite her, opened my laptop and clicked on a file of standard questions I'd prepared and which I would pretty much ask of everyone in the family. Settled, I then heard a litany of family history extolling one extraordinary Warriner after another, whether in the military or in politics, and noted the phrase *damn Yankee* used contemptuously more than once, while that modern obscenity *the nigras* was casually cast out even more.

It was as though nothing had changed since 1850, neither civil rights nor the wounds of war that slowly, and for the most part, had healed elsewhere in the nation. The Warriners themselves, needless to say, were painted by Aunt Sarah as America's only true first family, a fact that was not to be challenged in any way—not by the Rockefellers, the Bushes, the Roosevelts, the Kennedys, or anyone else. As for President Obama and his wife, Aunt Sarah's opinion was contemptuously expressed with, "That uppity pair who took over the White House never learned their place."

Taken back in spite of myself by the dismissive aggression of the old woman's onslaught against anyone who wasn't either Warriner or wasn't directly descended without taint from some Civil War great among its statesmen and warriors, it was not without a certain temerity that I asked about Candice.

A silence that lasted so long that I thought the old woman hadn't heard me was suddenly broken by two words almost spat out from between the withered lips. "Damned Creole!" And then two more words hissed out. "Like Celine. Half-breed slut. Two in our family. Shamed us."

I retreated. Clearly Candice, to say nothing of the long-dead Celine, was someone not to mention where Aunt Sarah was concerned. But the damage was done by my ever asking about them. The response to one last question was icy. When I asked her tactfully about the cause of her rejection of matrimony, thinking romantically and in spite of myself that there might be a broken-heart story there, I heard in a truculent and dismissive few words how a youthful engagement to marry had by necessity been broken off when it was discovered that the young man's social credentials were not equal to her own.

Chagrined for not having known better and thanking the old woman profusely for her time, I left her to her angry memories and petit point.

The interview, if you could call it that, left me a little shaken. Running into rampant racism on the job was something I hadn't envisioned. My second interview was to be with Charlotte, who had agreed to receive me right after Aunt Sarah. With one down and several more to go, I headed for the second Mrs. Warriner's private study. It was also was on the same floor, just two doors down a wide hall from Freddie's office and approached through an anteroom occupied by Miss Davies, who sat in a proprietary manner at a small desk on which there was a laptop. Close by was a copy machine and some file cases.

Charlotte's own desk was in the larger room beyond, which was entered through high, double doors with large brass French handles. Her ornate desk was bare save for a tray of expensive writing paper with accompanying envelopes, her laptop in a Moroccan-leather case decorated with the large gold-embossed letters *CW*, and next to a telephone, a thin booklet with a blue cover, which, I was to discover, was called the *Blue Book* and contained the names of one hundred people Charlotte considered worthy of her acquaintance. In it, along with the telephone number and email address of each entry, were the names of their husbands and children, their husbands' various alma maters and clubs to which they belonged, and their children's private schools.

The highly polished rectangular surface of a nearby table, the four delicate mahogany legs of which were line-inlaid with white boxwood, was replete with a collection of gilt-framed photos of various social functions along with group pictures of wealthy-looking society ladies whom, I was soon to learn, were the only people acceptable enough for the big bosomy Charlotte to associate herself with.

Prominently displayed on the table also were several copies of a glossy magazine titled *Delta Gatherings* and which featured, amidst glossy advertising for highly expensive products, those "acceptable ones" at all their various social functions.

After being announced by Miss Davies, I found Charlotte as difficult to talk to as Aunt Sarah. I saw right from the beginning that I was being tolerated only because what I was doing would enhance Charlotte personally. Finding a small chair, I sat in it directly cross the desk from her.

Sensing it was exactly what Charlotte wanted most to hear, I started right off and said, "I shan't be long. Just a few quick questions. If you think they are too personal, please just say so. Most people, I've found, don't particularly like talking about themselves," which I knew was such nonsense that I nearly gagged on it. "You've been married three years," I continued. "How did you come to know your husband?"

"What bearing does that have on the family today, Miss Henley?" The reply had a distinctly defensive tone.

Ouch, I thought and said as respectfully as I could, "It helps the general picture of the family to get a little background."

Charlotte smiled disparagingly. "People in our circle, Miss Henley, are generally all acquainted in one way or the other. Given the social standing of your own family, I'm sure you must find it the same in Baltimore."

"Oh, yes, of course, Mrs. Warriner," I quickly agreed and then checked my notes and asked, "Was Candice, his first wife, considered something of an obstacle?"

"Most definitely."

"Did you know Connors when he was married to her?"

There was a moment's silence, and looking up from my laptop I could have sworn Charlotte frowned. *I'm not going to get the truth on this one*, I thought, *if I get anything at all.*

I was right. She spoke suddenly, her voice heavy. "I don't see that question as relevant either, Miss Henley."

I decided to stay away from any personal questions and stick to the family and the sort of nonsense that's printed about celebrities in which their lives are always made to seem exemplary, and any untoward emotion or bad behavior explained away with tortured excuses about their sensitivity and talent. But whereas Aunt Sarah had been voluble about the Warriner family down through the years since the Civil War, it struck me as odd that Charlotte had little to say about them, nor anything much either about Lonsdale Hall, which was her home and of which she was the titular mistress. Her sole interest was clearly in the importance of her position in Louisiana society, which she was quite definite in letting me know about. And in spite of her understanding that I was there to publicize her with a flattering article in *Great American Families*, she was insufferably patronizing, unable to hide seeing me as being someone she thought had clearly abandoned respectability and become a traitor to her class for the lowly job of reporting and photography, a someone whom, because they were so fallen, she would have never allowed in the house except that their presence enhanced her own social prominence.

For me, her attitude came close to laughable, and there was good reason for my feeling that way. As I questioned the woman, I mentally clicked through what Jermyn Gutierrez had picked up about her. It was a background Charlotte had long and, I thought, often laboriously hidden and might explain, in part, at least, why she was so defensively aggressive. Her knowledge of what she thought was my own social background in Baltimore, that I'd led the family to believe, could possibly have made her feel a little fearful of possible discovery by someone who could spot flaws in what with her was a careful masquerade. Charlotte wasn't her real given name, and she'd hardly been born into society. Her birth certificate said her parents had called her Catherine, she'd been called Candy in school, and she'd originated in a Virginia social milieu far from her regal position in Louisiana. Her father had been a chiropractor, her mother a bridal-wear store manager. How Charlotte arrived at her current status was also something of a well-concealed mystery, but before surfacing in New Orleans, she had married twice, to increasingly wealthy and socially important men, a fact, given her looks, that raised questions.

Apparently at an early age, Gutierrez told me, she had been consumed with jealousy of girls who "had it all" when her high school competed in sports with an exclusive private school, and he'd said during one of my briefing sessions, "I suspect that she saw a way to getting their privileged lifestyle for herself by picking on men who had something to hide and employing the simple strategy of 'Marry me, or I'll tell all.'"

I wondered, right then, and while I interviewed her, was that the case with her marriage to Connors? It increased my suspicion, certainly, that there was indeed the suspected dark side to him that had brought me there. Pedophiles are more than aware that exposure to their sickness would mean complete ruination.

I took a half-dozen pictures that would flatter her, elaborately setting up my fake Canon, which, along with my wristwatch, recorded every word of our conversation while I surreptitiously took pictures with my iPhone. Then, glad finally to escape,

I thanked Charlotte profusely and packed up my things. On my way out, I almost collided with Miss Davies, the shapeless little woman with the pince-nez elbowing her way past in the doorway without a word as she bustled in with papers for Charlotte to sign.

Pausing in the small anteroom, I noticed a stack of pamphlets on her desk. Presuming that they were for distribution or had been at some time in the past, I helped myself to one, and back in the hall-way paused to look at it. It was for a Foundation, A Future for Girls, and displayed a page of colored photos of little girls in dire straits, their clothing in tatters, their unwashed hair limp, and their faces pale with want. A facing page compared them with fresh bright young things whom, the pamphlet said, the foundation's help would enable them to be like. A list of patrons followed, along with a state-ment as to the aims of the foundation that showed Charlotte as chairman.

I had hardly digested this information and had started down the hall intending to go downstairs when I found myself confronted by a simpering Ashley, who had obviously been listening at the door while I talked to Charlotte and who now fairly danced alongside of me as I headed for the guest room I occupied.

"Did Charlotte tell you all about this year's foundation fund-raiser? Did she? And do I see you snitched a pamphlet all about the little girls? It's this week, tomorrow, I think, or maybe the day after. She started it up three years ago, the moment Candice died and she took over, and now she has one every year. Millions of bratty little tweaks running wild everywhere and spilling ice cream all over themselves and everybody else. They're absolutely hateful. Miss Davies organizes it, of course, and does all the work, along with our servants, while Charlotte captures all the glory. A big picture in the society page and all that."

A bit taken back, I was trying to find words to reply when he said, "I bet she didn't tell you about Candice, though, did she?" Ashley's tone was malicious. "How she was already elbowing Candice out before she died? Oh, there was no question of that. She had her hooks into Connors long before the accident."

We had reached the head of the stairs that swept down to the marble hall below, and he said, "You know all about that, don't you? The accident. You must. It was front-page for months." He giggled. "And even on the TV news. We had them out here with all their trucks and paraphernalia for days, you know. You can't imagine. You couldn't walk out the front door without someone with a microphone rushing up. And then the police. Oh, my goodness. Sneaking around and asking everyone idiotic questions. You'd think there'd been a murder."

I managed eventually to shed him with a promise to photograph his tennis lesson. Gutierrez had thoroughly briefed me on the accident that in all its lurid details had ended the life of Connors's first wife. Candice was a waterskiing enthusiast, and Connors was towing her along the still waters of the Bayou Teche with his Chris-Craft when she fell. A loop of the tow rope had somehow snaked around her neck. Strangled, she was dragged several hundred yards at speed before Connors realized what had happened. The tabloid press had got onto the fact that Candice's and Connors's marriage was in trouble—perhaps one of the servants had talked— and had indulged in a field day of speculation and insinuation. It was months before it all died down and Connors and Charlotte could marry without being front-page.

With both Aunt Sarah and Charlotte out of the way, I locked myself in my room, and getting out my laptop and using the notes I'd made during both interviews, I wrote up all that had happened that day, encrypted it, and emailed it to Gutierrez.

Of course I was totally innocent of the FBI reaction to my email. Almost the moment he received it, Jermyn Gutierrez wasted no time in picking up his in-house phone and calling Tom Whitman, and they met at once in Tom's office one floor above.

Tom read the email Jermyn handed him, and when he put it down, he let out his breath in relief. "So. Hard to believe, but she's in. Accepted. And apparently nobody the wiser. Cross fingers it stays that way. Now to see what she turns up, if anything." He laughed. "Picked a winner, you old devil. You see right inside people sometimes. Calls for early quitting time today, Señor Gutierrez. C'mon, I'll buy you a drink."

Gutierrez allowed himself an inner smile of satisfaction.

NINE

My first report in, I remembered Felicity's saying she'd show me the gardens. *Flowers of any kind*, I thought, *even weeds, would be a blessed relief after the interviews.* It was still some time before dinner, and seeing the gardens with Felicity would get me out of having them shown by Ashley.

I found her in one of her favorite places, an air-conditioned glass-enclosed arboretum off one end of the house where there were flowers and additional cooling from a fountain. She was seated on a camp chair before her easel, and next to her there was a large potted azalea bush afire with pink blossoms that indicated what the mass of confused colors on her watercolor pad were a painting of.

As I watched her brushing on mixed-up colors, I almost envied her. In retreating somewhere into a world of her own fantasy, she managed to exclude the endless rejection by her family. Spiteful comments seemed to flow by her like the waters of a far-distant sea, and more and more she was beginning to stand out for me as the one socially acceptable person in a family in which social acceptance seemed to have an even greater importance than life itself.

"Hi, Felicity. You said you'd like to show me around the gardens."

"Do you like my painting?"

"I love it." And wondering if I might spoil my approval by perhaps going a little too far, I added, "I wish you'd do a special one for me sometime."

To my relief, Felicity's childish face broke into a smile. She put down her brush and said, "I can show you the whole property, too."

Perfect, I thought. And said, "Oh, Felicity, would you? I have nothing else to do at the moment, and I'd like so much to take pictures of everything."

"You don't have your camera."

"I'll use it later. I'll take sample pictures first with this." I pulled my iPhone from my shoulder bag.

"I used to take pictures with mine," Felicity said. "But Charlotte took it away from me."

"Oh? Why did she do that?"

"She said I had to learn to mind my own business."

I suddenly sensed I might be onto something more useful than the interviews I'd conducted. "Were you taking pictures of things you weren't supposed to?"

"It was pink and I painted some flowers on it."

This was seemingly unrelated to anything going on or being talked about, but I was getting used to that in Felicity. For a moment I thought the answer was deliberate evasion, but then I realized it was simply Felicity's childish mind flitting to something else. I said, "Pink with flowers? That sounds lovely."

Abandoning the easel and her camp chair, Felicity took me by the hand and led me from the arboretum. "Let's go this way," she said.

Felicity leading, we went across the front lawn encircled by the driveway, then through the lilac hedge and into a highly formalized garden that was laid out in eighteenth-century French style. A half-dozen busy Latino gardeners and grounds workers paid no attention to us.

"Missy says they're illegal," Felicity said as we stopped a moment to watch them, and I remembered that Connors had been outspoken during the last session of Congress in condemning any immigrants, legal or illegal, even those who were allowed in temporarily to harvest crops.

"And Charlotte said," Felicity added, "that if I told anyone, she'd take my paints away, too." Again a statement out of the blue, and perhaps the most number of words I'd heard from her since I'd arrived. I gave her shoulder a hug. I had an ally in Felicity, I knew, and it gave me a good feeling.

I asked her where the gardeners lived or if they just came by the day.

"In the old slave houses," Felicity said.

I remembered seeing some outbuildings at the end of the island in an aerial photograph, and wondered if they were what she meant, and asked her, but Felicity didn't answer, and still holding my hand, pulled me onward.

The gardens ended at the extensive acreage of what had once been cultivated and now was in nearly waist-high wild grass where once crops had grown.

Narrow bordering woods separated the field on both sides from the Bayou Teche so that the vast field was enclosed, and Felicity led us onto a paved path that started at the gardens and took us a short way across a corner of the field and through the wood on the field's right to the bayou, where we came upon a modern boathouse that was in stark contrast to Lonsdale Hall itself, and where a dozen pair of water skis stood in a rack, and a wooded dock on piles stretched out some twenty feet into the bayou. Resting in a boat cradle and pulled up on tracks set into a concrete ramp next to the dock was a sleek Chris-Craft speed boat, its cockpit and passenger areas covered with a carefully lashed-down tarp.

"That's Connors's boat," Felicity said. "He took Candice out waterskiing behind it and she died."

She stood quietly staring at it, and I was wondering what she was thinking—had she been there that day?—when she suddenly said, "I'm not allowed in it."

"You never get to ride in the boat?"

"Candice was in it, and I took a picture, and Charlotte took my iPhone from me."

With that, Felicity abruptly turned away and headed back up the path through the wood to the field, leaving my thoughts in a turmoil. Had Charlotte been around then, when Connors was still married to Candice and around enough to have felt she had the right to confiscate Felicity's iPhone? FBI research hadn't come up with that. If it were true, and given what I'd heard about Candice, that she and Charlotte were hardly friends, then it didn't seem likely that Charlotte would have come down to the boathouse to see Candice go off skiing.

I thought Felicity had to have had the days mixed up, and her iPhone confiscated on some other day much later, after Candice died and when

Charlotte, legitimately around, took it from her not because Felicity took a picture of Candice in the boat, as Felicity said, but for some other reason. Given Felicity's confused thoughts about so much, the answer had to be on Felicity's iPhone, but that was no help because Charlotte had it.

Then a second thought suddenly struck me, and forcibly. If perhaps Felicity did not have the days mixed up, and Charlotte had indeed been there, was it because she felt safe to be because she had gone past conspiring, as Ashley had intimated, to have Connors for herself, and already had her hooks into him, perhaps all the way?

I couldn't think further right then. The boathouse and all it represented depressed me. I hated any place where someone had died but stayed a moment and took several pictures, wondering as I did why no one except Felicity had offered to show me the boathouse and dock or, for that matter, had even mentioned them. It almost defied understanding. I'd come to publicize the Warriners—they thought so, at least—and from my first moment, not a one of them had offered to show me around. Except for Felicity. The thought emphasized to me my strange feeling that they were hiding something, all of them. And yet, represented by me, *Great American Families* had been invited to come. Was there something about me that had aroused some sort of animosity toward me personally? I couldn't think of anything, but the thought was worrying just the same.

I caught up to Felicity, and we continued across the field through the high grass to where it ended at another wood of giant southern live oaks, similar in their wide-spreading shape to those that flanked the front driveway and with the branches of some garlanded with Spanish moss. A path bordered with wildflowers led through them, and now clutching my hand again, Felicity led me determinedly along it. A brief walk and we came out onto another smaller field where the island tapered, and I saw down toward the end of it and crouched by the edge of the bayou six very old small brick houses that were no more than huts. The windows of all were open apertures without frames or glass, and there were the remains of fences around once yards in front of some, and on several the roofs had fallen in.

I shuddered. I knew perfectly well that they were the once slave quarters but just to make conversation, I asked Felicity. I said, "Good heavens, Felicity, what were these for?" I pointed my iPhone and took quick pictures.

"The nigras."

"Who?"

There was no answer. And I thought how per-fectly awful it was that a lovely childish person like Felicity was in all innocence using that terrible forbidden word. Just the way her spiteful old Aunt Sarah had done, but so knowingly. Racism with the Warriners certainly hadn't died with the poor devils who'd tilled the fields for them and brought great wealth into their lives. My thoughts flicked back to my days as a cop in New Orleans and the ever lingering racism there, and I thought, *Won't white people ever give it up?*

I heard Felicity suddenly say, "This is where the gardeners live."

"Here?" This time genuine surprise burst out of me involuntarily. "In these huts? But they're falling down, and can't possibly have any running water or sanitation in them."

Felicity didn't answer. I took a quick raft of shots, and then Felicity took my hand again, and we went through another relatively small wood at the field's end, and came out onto an open space at the very end of the island where it narrowed to a point and where, in a slight depression and almost hidden by saplings and brush, I saw another very old brick building. It was low and rather long and, like the slave huts, it looked abandoned for years. Part of the roof had fallen in at one end. There were no visible windows.

"What's that one, Felicity?"

"For when the nigras were bad."

There was a sudden difference in Felicity's tone, and I looked at her sharply. There was a glistening in Felicity's eyes. Tears? Perhaps racism hadn't touched her all the way.

We went to the building, pushing our way along a narrow track through the brush and saplings that were head high and almost hid a heavy wooden door that hung on long-rusted hinges. Felicity said, "Want to see?" and pushed it open, and I followed her into the one long room that was the entire interior. It was almost without light. Nesting birds, frightened by our entrance, fluttered away from rotting beams and out through the gaping hole in the roof, and I heard scurrying and rustling in the darkest corners. Rats.

The floor was dirt, and cobwebs covered nearly all the rafters, and whatever light there was I now saw came through the hole in the roof and though an open doorway at the building's far end that I hadn't been able to see from outside. Coming right up to it were the muddy waters of the bayou. The building would have to flood badly in any serious storm.

"Alligators come in that way," Felicity said, and even as she spoke, a fresh horror struck me. Along one wall were rusted, heavy, iron shackles on short chains attached to iron plates embedded in the brick, and farther back from the door and barely seen in the gloom, there were some rusty dog-size cages that were hung from a beam by chains.

I had only just imagined what they meant and the sheer awfulness of that, too, when I heard Felicity say, "It was right before Candice went skiing and died."

Oh, for heaven's sake! What was right before Candice went skiing? A moment's puzzlement, then, but of course, the picture she'd taken that got her iPhone confiscated by Charlotte. Felicity's childish mind had gone back to that.

And I was hit as though by electric shock with another thought. So Charlotte more than likely had been there just as Felicity said when Felicity took the picture of Candice. In fact, she must have been. And then was struck again, this time by an urgent question. What could have been so important about the picture to cause Charlotte to seize the camera that took it? Was there something in the picture she didn't want seen?

I didn't get a chance to think further. Felicity said, "Connors has some real old pictures of nigras in the cages, and there's one of a nigra chained up before an alligator came in and got him." And then almost immediately, and as though suddenly remembering, she said, "I'm not allowed in here. They'll take my paints away again."

Her voice tinged with fear, she pulled at me to follow her out, but before I allowed myself to be led away and remembering why I was there, I controlled my now shaky nerves and took quick photos with my iPhone of one of a pair of shackles about two feet apart and which were closest to the big door at the end where there was the most light. Each was secured when closed around a wrist or ankle by a threadless bolt dropped through a welded-on iron loop. Prisoners seated between a pair and fixed to them by their wrists would have been left with their arms raised up above their heads and unable to pull the bolts out and release the shackles, even with their teeth.

There'd been just enough light for me to notice a splotch of what seemed dried blood on the inner side of one, and though it didn't seem possible it looked as if it might have recently been used. I swung my iPhone around to take a picture of it and also pictures of the cages. Then, certain Felicity wouldn't understand what I was doing, I quickly rummaged in my camera tote bag for a tissue with which I reached up and wiped hard at the stain before slipping the tissue into a small, plastic bag and tucking it away back in the tote. I took a last shot of the rusty, hanging cages and then fled.

Closing the door behind me and Felicity as we left, I noticed with a start that its rusty hinges had been recently oiled. It confirmed my suspicion about the shackles. The dreadful place was still being used, but for what? Is that what the family seemed to be hiding? Something told me it was only the fabled tip of an iceberg. Wondering what would follow, I took a picture with my iPhone and followed Felicity away from it.

TEN

"Joanne, I'm having lunch in town with Charlotte," Freddie said. She adjusted a sun hat before the big Federalist mirror that hung over the long hall table. "But we'll be back for dinner. Connors has business in New Orleans and won't be home until tomorrow. Will you be all right with just Ashley and Aunt Sarah?"

"I'll be fine, Freddie," I said. "I have a lot of photography to do." It was the following morning and shortly after breakfast as I came into the hall with my photographic equipment.

"I'm afraid it will be mayhem the day after tomorrow," Freddie said. "But it could possibly be a photographer's field day for you. We're having the third annual foundation picnic party starting at about ten."

Charlotte, who had joined us, her usual dowdy self, clothed in yet another floral-print dress that was long out of style, looked displeased and said, "Joanne, Ashley tells me Felicity took you on a tour of the property. I hope you didn't see those dreadful old slave quarters?" Her tone was filled with embarrassment. Or was it disapproval?

Ashley misses nothing, I thought, and once again silently reminded myself to be careful of him. Trying to keep instinctive spite out of my voice, I quickly said, "They're so sad. I took pictures before we came back. Which we'll of course edit out of any article if you prefer not to publicize them."

Charlotte sniffed but Freddie laughed and said, "Print them if you want. They're all part of our history and a minor moneymaker. Tourists come up the Teche by the boat load to gawk at Lonsdale Hall and pay a price to the tour guide. We get a percentage from him."

To my relief, neither woman mentioned the slave jail, as I named it to myself, and it immediately occurred to me that they didn't want me to know it existed and had falsely presumed I'd not seen it because I hadn't mentioned it and, further, that they thought I'd come straight back to Lonsdale Hall after viewing the slave quarters.

But why shouldn't I know? Why hide it? I thought,

Then, remembering the oiled hinge, and Felicity's fear of being caught there, an ugly, second thought immediately followed; that maybe they didn't want me to know about the place because clearly, as I had guessed from the shackles and from what I thought might be blood on one, it was indeed still being used, although by whom and for what I couldn't at that moment imagine. Did Freddie or Charlotte know? Were they hiding something? It hardly seemed possible.

Watching them drive away down the long avenue arbored by the huge overhanging branches of the wide-spreading southern live oaks, I felt a shiver run through me. I was there to nail a possibly vicious criminal and to ferret out any connection with a sex-trafficking ring headquartered in the Far East. So far, and as an undercover agent, I was worthless. I'd only unearthed empty family tensions, social snobbery, and possible scandal. And yet from the first moment when I'd intuitively felt everyone was hiding something, I could not help but feel that given a little more time, someone would say or do something that would give me a clue as to what it was and might possibly put my investigation on the track it was supposed to be on.

I took a host of required pictures and then went to lunch, where I suffered old Warriner falling asleep while being spoon-fed, now by Missy. I had soon fallen in love with the dark, diminutive old woman whose snow-white hair lent a gentleness to her frail being and who had a wisdom in her eyes that made me feel I had met a sympathetic someone of true worth, and other than Felicity, probably the only one at Lonsdale Hall who was. I resolved to have a long talk with her as soon as I could arrange it. I wanted to talk, too, with Erik. The butler, silently going about his duties, had modernism written all over him, both in facial expressions and body language. He was big and powerful, and one could easily imagine him an NFL quarterback or a celebrity actor—and I wondered how and why he suffered employment with such racist people that was so servile and demeaning. Like the Warriners themselves, their servants, I thought, seemed to be hiding something.

Lunch finally over, Lonsdale Hall saw Aunt Sarah taking her regular after-lunch two hour rest, Miss Davies back at work making last-minute arrangements for the forthcoming foundation picnic, and Ashley again on the tennis court for his weekly lesson with Dennis the Tennis, the pro who had come out from Baton Rouge. The house was silent, and deciding this was an ideal time to snoop, I headed for my first target, old Warriner's study. Not far from the dining room, it had been used, I'd been told, by old Warriner himself, for strictly personal matters when home and away from his office at the State House and was now a shut-up stuffy place where blinds were drawn and dust cloths covered the furniture as if to emphasize that in reality he no longer existed.

Closing the door behind me, I began an extensive and silent search, but my efforts everywhere produced nothing but dust, empty desk drawers, and one file case without files of any kind in it. I thumbed rapidly through old calendars stacked on a corner table and came up zero there as well. And when I found neither telephone nor address books, I gave up and went on to my next target, the library.

Not far from the dining room, it was a small room, as rooms in Lonsdale House went, and was replete with priceless antebellum Federalist furniture and a plethora of paintings. It was darkened by heavy drapes shutting out most of the bright day, while the elaborate and heavily-fringed shades that adorned candelabras and table lamps were almost guaranteed to keep any light from escaping from low-wattage bulbs. Three walls were heavily decorated with ornately framed oval pictures of various long-gone mistresses of the house and by faded samplers exhibiting biblical quotes.

The fourth wall was entirely dominated by a large oil painting of a Confederate cavalry charge set in a massive heavily gilded frame. The officer who led the charge, sabre raised and leaning forward aggressively in the saddle of a great white war horse, was the revered family founder, I'd been told by Aunt Sarah. "Colonel Brigham Lee Warriner," she'd said, "was the undisputed greatest hero of the South's heroic defense against the North."

My first target, quite different from the rest of the furnishings, was an unlocked gun case in a far corner that caught my eye and in which I found six vertically racked shotguns, one clearly well maintained and quite recently used. Surprised that pudgy Congressman Connors shot—he didn't look the type—I went on to a mahogany secretariat that was topped by glass doors enclosing several shelves of expensive leather-bound volumes, which, belying the name of the room, contained what seemed the library's only few books.

After carefully rifling through drawers, it was clear that one of its users had been Candice. There were handwritten letters to and from friends, postcards she'd received, old address books, and a number of carefully stored calendars from past years when she was alive. There was evidence, too, of its current or recent use by both Ashley and Connors. There were separate boxes of personalized stationary embossed with their names in raised gold type as well as an expensive pen and pencil set with an inscription that said it was gifted to Connors by the grateful New Iberia Water Board. Other than a calendar of major worldwide tennis events, there was nothing more than normal items in the smaller drawers, such as paper clips, Post-Its, and Scotch tape. I turned my attention to the shelves above.

The books there were works of classic fiction, none of which appeared to have ever been opened. They were clearly for display only. I riffled through the pages of several to make certain nothing had been hidden in them, and a little dispirited at not finding anything, I turned my attention next to a low glass-fronted book case that boasted only a half-dozen photo albums. Opening the first three in order, I found myself looking at scores of typically bad family photos of the current occupiers of Lonsdale Hall during bygone years, as Arthur, Ashley, Connors and Felicity emerged slowly from infancy to childhood and then to adulthood, while Aunt Sarah and old Warriner aged equally.

The photos in the fourth album were relatively current. There were pictures of Candice, who, young and with the face and figure of an athlete, seemed a true modern Southern beauty and, compared to all others in the family, vivacious and charismatic.

The last two albums caught my eye as different from the first four. Their covers were slightly shabby, and they appeared to have been opened not only recently but quite often. I took out one of them, and what I saw at first were pictures, taken many years ago and faded with age, that were of the family who had occupied Lonsdale Hall during the Civil War which Charlotte chose, as did Aunt Sarah and many in the Deep South, to still call the War between the States. There were women in their finery, men looking gallant and proud in Confederate officers' uniforms.

And then the album turned to those unfortunates who had made such a storied life possible—the household slaves and the farm laborers, all staring at the camera with the numb expressions and dull eyes of people in whom hope had been long extinguished. Scattered among them were horror pictures—several of a shirt-sleeved white whipping a slave who was trussed up and bent over a barrel with a score of slaves assembled to watch. There was a picture, too, of the corpse of a slave who had received ultimate punishment. It dangled from a branch of one the great oaks flanking the driveway as, shockingly, a carriage bearing unconcerned beribboned ladies drove past, and finally there were several pictures of slaves shackled to the wall of the jail I had seen with Felicity. Feeling nothing but horror, my hands shaking, I put the album back and forced myself to snatch out and open the last one.

When I had recovered from what I then saw in that one, I steeled myself and with my iPhone took picture after picture of the relatively up-to-date photographs displayed over a dozen pages. They made a valuable record. Some were of Old Warriner in better days and dressed in the white robes of a grand master of the Ku Klux Klan. Others were pictures of burning crosses, and there were recent photos of Congressman Connors with Klan members and several more of him with brown-shirted neo-Nazi white nationalists standing before a big swastika flag, besides which there was a large picture of Adolf Hitler.

Bad enough had been my discovery of rampant racism in the Warriner family, this further evidence almost numbed me. I was appalled. Hiding behind a front of so-called respectability, these were people consumed, as though by their own fiery crosses, with hatred for anyone and everyone who was not like them. Given the chance, they would deport anyone not pure white, like the FBI's Jermyn Gutierrez or the Baton Rouge Agency chief, Tom Whitman—men who had devoted their lives to the very freedoms that allowed them to think the sickening way they did. And, suddenly aware of my own Osage heritage, I knew that they would even deport me too, or confined me to a reservation if they knew of my mixed blood.

I put the album away and tried to control my feelings over what I'd seen—the realization of what sort of people the Warriner family actually were. It was hard to get a grip on myself, and I had to forcibly concentrate on my not being there to judge their character or morals, no matter what they were. I was there to uncover, if it existed, possible pedophilia by Congressman Connors and, along with it, suspected ties to an international sex-traf-ficking ring. I was a cop on a case who so far had come up with nothing.

I was standing there struggling with myself when I was jarred back into reality by a now all too familiar voice. "Snooping around, are you?" I had done the unforgiveable; I had not paid atten-tion and hadn't registered that the sound of tennis I'd heard when coming in had ceased, which meant tennis was over and Ashley free to shadow me.

He had entered the library silently, and when I turned sharply, I saw he wore his usual simpering smile. My heart pounded. Had he seen me looking at the album? If he had, it could jeopardize my being there. I somehow kept my cool. "I hardly think," I said, managing a pleasant smile, "that doing my job was snooping. I see some photo albums. Are they worth my time, or are they just the same boring bunch of pictures every family has?"

I was answered by something of an effeminate giggle. And then, "When are you going to photo-graph me playing tennis?"

"How about tomorrow?"

Ashley quickly summoned up an expression and words of disparaging cruelty. "Bring Felicity, and we'll make it doubles."

I didn't dignify that nasty with a response. Instead I asked him, "Who in the family shoots? Connors, I suppose? One of those shotguns in the case was recently cleaned and oiled."

"Connors? Oh, no such luck. He used to, until Charlotte took over. Now it's her. *Pop! Pop! Pop!* And another sparrow or crow, or whatever she chooses, bites the dust in the garden. And, mind you, nothing like also parading around with a shotgun to keep the gardeners in line. So be sure you stay on the right side of Annie Oakley Warriner."

He took fake aim at me and said, "Or, *Pop! Pop!*" Then with yet another giggle at his own misguided humor, he virtually wisped away without further word, leaving me to think, *How horrid can you get,* and to utter a sigh of relief and abandon the library in turn once I was sure I wouldn't run into him again.

The appalling racism I'd discovered, Ashley's unexpected appearance as well as learning that Charlotte, of all people—although I suppose it suited her domineering masculine character—was the shooter, had slightly unnerved me. I had work to do, however, and decided, if possible, not to let anything stop me. I thought that perhaps the most important room was the one to go to next.

That was Connors's. It was close to Aunt Sarah's, and I went upstairs, and with her still having her nap and hopefully sound asleep, I kept an eye out for Ashley and tried the door. Once inside and the door closed behind me, I doubted, if I was silent, that he would enter the room. But the door was locked.

I was good at locks; they had always intrigued me, and I'd once read up on them and visited a locksmith's to find out more. Most of them are easily picked, and when a cop, I was always called on to open doors a fellow cop couldn't. I got out a toothpick-thick length of hard steel with a little hooked end from my camera bag and went to work. But no luck. It was an antiburglar one that couldn't be picked all that easily. It would take more time than I had at the moment. Interesting, but more interesting than a special lock was, why lock his bedroom at all? What was he hiding from family and servants?

Frustrated, I thought, *Okay, Charlotte next, then.*

But at the same time wondered if I should bother. What on earth could Charlotte possibly have hidden away, or even just lying about, that could incriminate her husband with pedophilia? And again, I had to remind myself not to judge prematurely, and of Gutierrez saying I should leave no stone unturned, even if it proved useless. "When you're on a search, Kasie, search everywhere, regardless," he'd said. "As a detective you should know that."

And of course I did. "So, never mind stalling

about," I said to myself. And added cryptically, "Get busy, *Joanne.*"

I remembered that Charlotte had a suite of rooms that were separate from Connors's. It was just down the hall from where I stood. *Some marriage,* I thought. I glanced at my watch, the one that also recorded voices. I still had time. Freddie and Charlotte weren't due back for another hour; Connors not at all. Felicity would be painting flowers someplace, Miss Davies had gone for the day, and the maids had already done up all the rooms. There was only Ashley still to worry about. He was no longer playing tennis, and doing anything with him on the loose was taking a chance, but my time at Lonsdale Hall was limited and I couldn't not work because of him. With the house almost ominously dead silent, I went down the hall and into Charlotte's room.

ELEVEN

Do bedrooms necessarily reflect the personality of their occupier? I decided they didn't. I saw nothing in Charlotte's bedroom that matched the individuality of the big bosomy woman and her loud floral-print dresses. The antebellum Federalist decor was reliably the same as in virtually all the other bedrooms in the rest of the house, and here I saw not a personality but just the same four-poster bed, the same style of dresser, the same lighting and drapery.

To my surprise, there were few personal items evident either in the bedroom or the bathroom, with its huge tub on four legs and its very ancient raised commode. At first sight, the place seemed unused. I found a toothbrush, and a hair dryer, and shampoo. Were they there for appearances' sake, because I saw no dressing gown or bathrobe hanging up, or even evidence of a nightgown or pajamas, and no sign of any medicine or anything that had to do with a woman's makeup? Could it be that Charlotte was actually sharing Connors room with him, and this room just for some distorted sense of Victorian show? They were married, but somehow I couldn't imagine Connors sharing a bed with such a woman. Or her, equally, sharing a bed with such a man. A search of his room later, when I had more time to get at the lock, would tell me what their personal relationship was, if anything, as well as the possibly incriminating evidence against him that I was at Lonsdale Hall to get.

Readying camera equipment and putting my Canon on a tripod so as to look as though I was taking legitimate photos for *Great American Families,* I began to look around. I knew my time was limited. I could handle that, but Ashley remained a constant danger—it seemed as though he was everywhere, all the time—worse luck. Or one of the maids could pop up.

I was busy gearing up a phony appearance of photography when I suddenly remembered Felicity's iPhone that Charlotte had confiscated, causing Felicity so much distress. Could it be here, in Charlotte's room? And at the same time, I realized that if it was here—and it might well be, because where else would Charlotte keep it except her office?—and if I found it, I couldn't give it back to Felicity without revealing that I'd been snooping.

But then I remembered, too, why Charlotte had confiscated the iPhone. It was because Felicity had been taking pictures of Candice and the Chris-Craft before Candice was towed to her death, and I was as sure of that now as I had been when at the boathouse. Charlotte was trying to hide something. Could it possibly be anything relating to why I was here? Probably not. But if it did, then the question was, what? It was infuriating. I felt close but also so far from whatever, and I had the incessant feeling that the elusive whatever was important, perhaps critically so.

I told myself to be patient. Investigating required it and required, too, going after the far-fetched, even if it seemed likely it would lead nowhere. I started with the most obvious places: the dresser where I found nothing but the minimum—a few underclothes, sweaters and stockings, all neatly folded, some in tissue which showed that they were not often used. The desk and its several drawers revealed nothing, either. *But they most likely wouldn't,* I thought, *because of the maids who might spot it and innocently return it to Felicity, not knowing it had been confiscated.*

There were no closets in the room, only a giant

walnut wardrobe that was virtually empty, its clothing bar only half occupied by a few floral-print dresses along with a similar number of skirts and blouses.

Well, wrong again, I thought. *Perhaps this is indeed the room she actually uses, and except for what? Sex? I doubt it.* And at the same time I saw that clearly Charlotte wasn't one to have feelings about fashion or, for that matter, how her utter lack of taste in clothes might appear to others. Nobody could wear what Charlotte wore without being smugly satisfied that she made a good appearance regardless. Her lack of taste didn't fit with her being a social snob, but then I knew that she hadn't been raised as one, and that good taste, like habits, was usually formed early in life. Clearly her parents were the source of her being so.

A dozen neatly arranged shoes boxes were on the wardrobe's bottom shelf. More of the same, I thought, and started to turn away, but then heard Gutierrez's voice in my inner ear again, and didn't. Kneeling, and after casting a slightly worried look at the doorway to the room—I realized I'd been there perhaps dangerously too long—I felt in each shoe, then turned to half a dozen shoe boxes.

I'd been through four of them, meticulously unwrapping tissue from each shoe that I found then meticulously rewrapping each one, and I was getting more and more stressed-out nervous and beginning to think I was wasting time, when my fingers, probing one of a pair of walking shoes, as tasteless as all of Charlotte's other clothing, felt a familiar object.

An iPhone. I pulled it out and was rewarded with a scramble of mixed-up bright colors, mostly various shades of pink that decorated its back.

The sudden sound of voices, one of them Aunt Sarah's, nearly panicked me until I realized the old lady would have no reason to come into Charlotte's room, and was probably only being brought tea by the maid who looked after her personally. But the forever following me Ashley? I hurriedly rewrapped the shoe, stuffed the iPhone into my camera equipment bag, closed up the wardrobe, picked up my Canon on its tripod, and headed for the door.

I found it half blocked by an incoming Ashley, and I had only one immediate thought: *Oh, my God, I knew it.*

"Taking more pictures? I'm sure they'll look nice, since Charlotte isn't in the room."

Almost overwhelmed with relief that he hadn't caught me at the shoe boxes, I collected my senses and thought I'd try one on. I said as casually as possible, "You don't like her much, do you?"

"Do you? Does anybody?" Ashley giggled and added, "Tit for tat, Right? Charlotte doesn't like any of us, either."

I decided to switch. This was interesting. "How

did everyone get along with Candice?"

"Candice? Splendidly. She was gorgeous, and such a fireball. The exact opposite of Charlotte. Everyone loved her. Everyone except Connors, that is."

"Oh? Like that, was it?"

Ashley giggled again. "Worse. She had his number and he couldn't stand it."

"Had his number in what way?"

"Putting himself out as a big deal when he wasn't. All his congressional nonsense, which is usually a front for something else—like doing nothing," he laughed, "or running down to New Orleans for some sort of frivolous night out with friends. Not that he has many. And boasting about running Delta Red when Freddie has always done it for him. Just like she did for the old boy before he became a cauliflower." Ashley took a breath. "Candice put up with him until Amelie Faure."

"Who?" Alert bells rang in me. From somewhere way back in my police days the name was familiar.

"Amelie Faure."

"Who's she?"

Ashley smirked. "You don't know Amelie? Oh, but then you're a girl; I almost forgot the way you tote all those cameras up and down. Amelie provides beautiful young things for all the politicians when their wives aren't around." He giggled.

"I heard she provides for some of the wives, too, if they're the kind who like that sort of thing."

Of course, I thought, finally remembering her well. She was all the billionaires' favorite madam. Aloud, I said, "An escort service?"

Ashley's smirk grew more pronounced. "You might call it that."

"And Candice caught Connors with someone?"

"More like half a dozen. Amelie provided him with kinky stuff, too."

I felt a jab of real interest. "Kinky stuff? What kind of kinky stuff?"

He giggled, "All kinds, I guess. You know, anything that pleases a kinky mind."

Dead end. I was trying to think how to recover when he said, "I heard Candice was well on her way out when she saved Connors a small settlement fortune by having the *accident.*"

"Were you there? I mean when the accident happened?"

"I was playing tennis."

The way he said it, along with his smirk, told me that he had been there and was lying. That was interesting. Why should he be?

I decided to change tack again. "Ashley, what do you do besides play tennis?" I almost added "and skulk around after me," but somehow managed not to.

I was rewarded with the inevitable smirk. "I

don't do anything, thank you. I don't have to, do I?"

"Don't you?"

"When the cauliflower decides to do us all a favor and wilts all the way, I get a third of Delta Red."

"And Connors and Felicity the same?"

'Yes, such the pity. I suppose Felicity will buy a paint company with hers unless Connors figures some way to cheat her out of it. I'm for Tuscany, the Amalfi Drive. All those gorgeous young Italians." Another pointed giggle at the thought of such hedonistic pleasure. "Anything but this morgue."

Further information from Ashley was brought to a halt by the sound of Charlotte and Freddie returning. Their voices, Charlotte's loud and masculine, floated upward from the front hall.

"Oh, dear." Ashley squeaked. He turned to go and stopped and said, "This room is just for show. Charlotte sleeps in Connors's room so as to watch naughty forbidden things on the Internet with him, and also to not let a single night go by without her bullying him into doing whatever she wants. Nag, nag, nag. He really hates her."

And was off.

So was I. I thought, *Wow, forbidden things on the Internet?* That meant porn, what else? And given what Connors was suspected of probably even child porn. I thought, *Bit by bit, things always crawl from under flat rocks,* and I packed up hurriedly and went to my room, closing the door behind me.

Locked in the bathroom, I extracted Felicity's iPhone from my camera tote bag. I was going to need a password, and tried to think of a very simple one that Felicity could remember. I'd decided on the word *paint* and also the word *picture,* and then found her iPhone opened automatically and supposed, remembering Charlotte saying Felicity wasn't allowed email, that they had eliminated a password so they could review whatever she had on it without the bother of one.

It didn't take me long to bring up her picture album. There were shots of everything, along with dozens of nothingness when Felicity must have pointed the camera at the sky or at the ground. Some pictures were of individuals: of Freddie, of Missy, of Candice looking radiant. Some were of Ashley and Connors, and there were several of old Warriner before his wheelchair days. At first, there were none of Charlotte. *She clearly doesn't like Charlotte,* I thought.

But then I suddenly came to a picture Felicity said she had taken by the boathouse, and Charlotte was indeed in it, as was Candice, who, in a wetsuit and clutching water skis, was stepping into the Chris-Craft where Connors was already at the wheel. Felicity had not got her days mixed up, and so much for Charlotte ducking my question of how long she'd known Connors. The answer, unlikely as it seemed, was obviously quite a while.

A second picture showed the Chris-Craft surging away, Charlotte waving after it. I stared. Something in that picture was terribly wrong. It took a moment, and then I suddenly thought I knew why Charlotte had confiscated the iPhone. Candice hadn't died with her neck caught in the tow rope. That couldn't have happened because Ashley was in the shot, too—so much for his saying he was playing tennis—and so was old Missy. They were both coming out of the boathouse, Missy with an armful of towels and Ashley with the coiled tow rope in hand and holding it up and waving at the departing Chris-Craft as though to tell Connors and Candice they had forgotten something.

Bu t I held down any excitement. I had spent enough time in court on one police matter or another that if I'd learned nothing, I'd learned that to win cases, prosecutors could leave no area of doubt as to the guilt of the accused. And like it or not, and on second thought, reasonable doubt was raised by Felicity's picture.

The picture was damming but only if taken on the very day Candice was said to have died, strangled by the tow rope. She could have died, I realized, on a day other than the one in Felicity's picture, and thus the picture entirely circumstantial, even though Felicity said it was the reason her iPhone was taken away from her.

I cross-checked with my encrypted file of data on every member of the Warriner family. I pulled the file on Candice and checked the date of her death. It matched the date on the photo. Guilty? Looked it. But wait. Still not proof.

For if she had died that day, suppose that a few minutes after the photo was taken, Connors had realized he had no tow rope, and had come back to get it. There was only the one picture of him taking off in the boat with Candice. Any good defense attorney would have brought that up, and if he didn't, the jury would.

Dead end. It had paid me not to leap with excitement.

There was another question, too, I thought, that any seasoned defense attorney worth his salt would have raised. Could everyone in the picture I saw actually have been complicit in hiding a murder? All of them—Connors, Charlotte, Ashley? All three? I excluded Missy. Accusing her stretched the imagination. Defense would have used the near impossibility of group complicity or even guilt, especially by such a prominent and famous family, to prove his client's innocence. A jury would see in the family's innocence proof of no malfeasance on the part of the defendant. Thus again, no proof of murder. And yet—my thoughts went back to my impression when I'd first met them, gathered like a mafia reception committee, that they were all hiding something, and that left me, crazily enough, not absolutely certain of group innocence and with the thought that they might well be hiding, in addition to their white nationalist views, knowledge of a murder, if not complicity in the murder itself.

At that moment, however, there could only be suspicion by me or anyone else that either Connors Warriner alone had murdered Candice, or that he'd had help through the silence of his family. It was realistically hard to think otherwise, and trying not to dwell on it any longer, I had to forcibly to tell myself once more to let it go for the moment. I wasn't there to pursue a murder, if in fact there really had been one. I'd report what I'd found to the Baton Rouge police when I got back, and leave it to them to pursue the matter.

I started to put the iPhone away in my camera bag and then didn't. Regardless of my good intentions, something nagged; a thought that I had at first ignored but now became increasingly insistent. There was no proof of murder. But suppose for a moment my first thought, regardless of no proof, was right—that Connors Junior had indeed murdered his wife.

If so, then a question begged. *Why* would he have? What would have been his motive? Most people, I thought, didn't risk murder to get rid of a wedded partner. If they couldn't reach an amiable agreement, they sued and went to court. Had there been more going on here than a bad marriage? Was there some reason he would have felt compelled to take such a risk?

Time spent investigating criminal cases surged up in my memory. I remembered that when I was still a rookie, the veteran cop I'd been teamed up with had said half the murders he'd ever worked on had been committed to shut the victim up because the victim had knowledge of something that was lethally dangerous to the killer.

It was right then, and in remembering, that it struck me I was possibly onto something connected with my being at Lonsdale Hall after all. Conjecture, maybe, or a so-called hunch, but I'd always felt the stab of excitement I suddenly felt now because I'd stumbled on a truth. In this case the truth could be that odious pedophilia was a motive for murder. What better reason for Connors's marriage to Candice to go rocky than if he was indeed the pedophile we suspected he was, and she knew of his sickness and threatened to betray him? What better reason for him to then murder her to avoid exposure, certain ruin, and prison?

I felt a cold shiver of revulsion. The suspicion,

raised by a *New York Times* investigative reporter, of possible twisted depravity in the congressman could well turn out to be more than just suspicion. "Girls to be …" could indeed mean child-girls of interest to a sick mind. I'd been so involved with the unexpected quirkiness of the Warriner family that I had almost lost sight of that. Now I no longer did.

Reality clung to me like some sickening filth. I had met and dined with the suspect, shaken his hand, talked to him one-on-one. I slept under the same roof as he, and I had yet to formally interview him, to get quotes from him for the theoretical article in *Great American Families.* I suddenly hated the job and wished I'd never agreed to do it.

Then, and even as I was swept by a wave of anger on hearing Charlotte's masculine voice as the big woman came down the corridor to her room, I was struck by another thought—did Charlotte also know the monster her husband might be? Had she held that over him to force him into a marriage that for her would be the ultimate in social triumph she had for so long yearned for? In her nights in his locked room did she use watching the "forbidden" on the Internet with him—as Ashley had insinuated—as a way to constantly stimulate his sick predilection to her advantage?

I found dinner that evening a nightmare. Keeping up a front of innocence was exhausting. Sleep that night was difficult. My only comforting thought was that if I was on the right track, if Connors was the monster I was pretty sure he was, and if Charlotte *was* a fraudulent extortionist of the worst sort and an equal monster, they would have no interest in me. I was just a little reporter taking pictures and telling the story of how wonderful they were. I was as safe as rain. Unless they somehow found out who I really was and what I was really there for.

TWELVE

Before going to bed the night, I again emailed a full encrypted report to Gutierrez of my daily observations to date along with many of Felicity's photos as well as my conclusions about Candice's death and Charlotte's presence as the second Mrs. Warriner. Both, I thought, supported suspicion that Connors might well be a pedophile. Shortly before finally turning out the light, I'd heard Connors returning from wherever he'd been and tried not to imagine where that was and what he might have been doing. And tried, also, not to dwell on the sickening thought that I still had to interview him to keep up appearances as a photo-journalist for *Great American Families.*

At breakfast the next morning, I summoned up my courage, managed somehow to look at him with a smile and said, "Connors, I've interviewed everyone except you. Can you spare a half an hour?"

I waited, forcing myself not to avert my eyes from his appearance, his slickly polished bald head that seemed to have no neck below it, his coldly arrogant lusterless eyes, his puckered immature mouth that was more often than not set in a pouting semi-sneer that lent his whole expression cruelty.

After what seemed an eternity, Connors slowly raised his eyes from a sheaf of official letters he'd brought to the table to read while he ate. "It'll have to wait," he said. After that he didn't speak further. Charlotte, her heavy face still filled with sleep, spoke for him. "My husband has an important meeting to attend at the State House and must leave the moment he's finished eating. Perhaps some other time?"

It was said with such authority and in a tone so oddly warning as to virtually be a statement that Connors was not to be interviewed, ever. The nagging impression I'd begun to have, that in spite of all his cold chauvinistic arrogance Connors was completely dominated by his big bosomy wife, was reinforced in me, and I was again swept with the chilling thought that if Connors had indeed murdered Candice, then Charlotte could well have been the mind behind it.

With my iPhone already loaded with scores of pictures of everything both within and outside Lonsdale House, I realized I'd missed one vital part of the place—Missy. The dear old woman had to be a trove of information for the record in *Great American Families,* and off the record have helpful information that could support the suspicion against Connors as well. So, breakfast over, I caught old Missy emerging from Warriner Senior's room with a tray of half-finished eggs and toast.

"Missy, you're my next interview," I said, taking the tray abruptly from frail old hands. *But where,* I wondered. The library was the obvious choice, but I was sure Missy would feel uncomfortable there with the certain possibility of either Charlotte or Ashley appearing unexpectedly. Or perhaps even Freddie. "Your room," I said, quickly, making up my mind. "We can drop the tray off in the kitchen on the way," and without giving Missy a chance to protest, I steered her straight for the kitchen, shoving the tray into the hands of a startled scullery maid, who stared at me with wide and frightened eyes, and propelling Missy out the back kitchen door to the servants' low building that was hidden behind the main house by a high hedge of arborvitaes.

The comparison between the small yellow-brick building that housed the servants who took care of the historic antebellum opulence of Lonsdale Hall, along with all the physical needs and luxuries of its owners, was even worse than I expected. The door opened immediately on a sort of common room where the servants were able to watch television on a very old set boasting less than a twelve-inch screen. Along with the TV, there were only two cheap wooden chairs, a rickety table that belonged to no period, and an ancient sagging couch, its springs coming up through its upholstery, its cushions in tatters.

In the kitchen that vied in drear, bare grease-stained walls encircled an ancient refrigerator, a three-burner coal stove, and shabby linoleum-covered counters. But both rooms were an improvement over the six small bedrooms above that were reached by a narrow unlit staircase.

Missy's room, which I had to virtually force the old woman to take me to, was as coldly shabby and unwelcoming as the rooms downstairs. There was a sagging iron bed with an overly worn mattress, a table with a shadeless lamp, and an unpainted two-drawer dresser. In the absence of either wardrobe or a closet, Missy's few clothes—three well-worn dresses and a threadbare coat for winter wear— were hung along with a ragged sweater—out at both elbows—on hooks along one wall.

While Missy stood in anxious and confused silence, I firmly closed the door behind us and sat myself down on her bed. "Missy, come sit next to me." I patted the space beside me. "Come!" Authoritatively. And when Missy, with hesitant reluctance, finally did, I said, "You know who I am and why I am here, surely. Someone must have told you. Part of my job is to interview everyone in the family. I've done that. Now it's your turn. I'm going to ask you questions, and please try to answer them as best you can. Let's start with what I know about you. You lost both your parents when you were very young, and when you were ten, someone—did Freddie tell me it was an agency for orphaned children? Yes?—found you a home with the Warriner family washing dishes and mopping the floors. Is that right?"

The answer was silence. Missy, eyes averted and twisting her hands in her lap, stared across the room at nothing.

This, I thought, *is going to be rough.*

And it was. But over an hour later, when I left after giving Missy a warm hug and kiss and leaving her with fifty dollars to buy herself "something nice" the next time she went to town, because it had come out that Missy hadn't been paid in years, a file in my iPad was filled with what I had learned.

For eventually Missy had talked, hesitantly at first with only the wary platitudes of a trusted family servant; the Warriners were beyond reproach and nothing was revealed that I hadn't already learned either from my briefings and preparation for the job or from interviewing or observation since I'd arrived.

I'd kept probing, however, asking the elderly woman for more and more, and my experience in interrogation as a police officer paid off. As Missy became used to gentle questioning and lulled by my already gained knowledge not only of the family but of herself, she became less and less on her guard and began to feel more and more confident.

And as she talked, I took in every word on my Canon camera recorder and backed it up with the recorder on my little wristwatch.

My bringing up Candice and her death proved a final key to unrestrained talk. Missy had clearly been very attached to Connors's first wife, and without further urging she suddenly poured out a wealth of information in a flood of words mixed with tears. She held nothing back, and I learned to my shocked surprise that Erik was Missy's son by old Connors Warriner, who had raped her repeatedly when she was barely in her teens, summoning her to his study at night when his wife was asleep along with the rest of the household and when he had said he needed to work late.

"Wasn't nothin' I could do to stop him, Miss Henley. Had to let him have his way or be turned out into the street and work in one of them New Orleans bad houses," Missy said. "Then when Erik, he growed up a little and someone tol' him what that old man had done to his mama and that he was Erik's father, Erik, he went crazy like, and stole some silverware to sell so as to set me and him up someplace out of here. But he went and got caught at it, and old Warriner tol' him if'n he didn't keep workin' he'd turn him in to the police and make sure he'd do ten years and maybe more, 'n he said he'd do me in with him, sayin' I was in it with my son. 'N before he got silly in the head, he done told his son, 'n Connors, he's been holdin' it still over Erik's head ever since to make him stay here along with me and keep me out of the poorhouse for no-good black people."

I managed to swallow my feelings. I didn't dare tell the dear old woman that her days at Lonsdale Hall might be coming to an end, that the Warriner family, who had so tormented her and her son for so long, might in turn find themselves in an even greater torment of their own making. I gently got her around to the day Candice died in the waterski-ing accident. Had she been there?

"Oh, yes, Miss Henley. Missy done bin there all right." She'd come down to the dock, she said, with a sweater for Miss Candice to put on after she'd finished skiing because she was certain Miss Candice would be cold from the water, even though it was a hot day. When Candice had died, she said she couldn't believe the story about her getting tangled in the tow rope and strangling, "because there wasn't no tow rope to tow her with, 'cause Mister Connors he'd done left it in the boathouse, and Mister Ashley, he was runnin' to give it to him, but he already done took off with her in the boat. He'd forgot it, that's what it was. There wasn't no rope in that boat 'n he was real queer that day because of all the fightin' with her several nights before."

"What fight, Missy? Tell me."

"They'd started it in their bedroom," Missy said, "shoutin' and cursing each other somethin' terrible. We could hear them all the way back here where we live. Mostly at first it was about Miss Charlotte and why was she there and Miss Candice demandin' he get rid of her right away and accusin' Miss Charlotte of tryin' to take her place. 'N then it was about somethin' terrible he'd done to some little girl, too."

"Some little girl?"

"Yes, ma'am. That's what she said, and Connors, he wasn't denyin' it no way."

And then Missy told how they'd gone to the boathouse so they wouldn't be heard. But, before they did, Missy, unable to sleep from their row, had gone out to the garden to sit on a bench by the boathouse path and enjoy the cool night air, and had soon found herself again an unwilling and frightened listener to everything said.

Connors had some photos he'd taken of some little girl, Missy didn't know who, only that Candice said she'd found them on his iPhone and made copies of them onto hers, and that she would hand them to the police if Connors didn't give her a divorce and a half of Delta Red in settlement.

Connors's anger had been terrible, Missy told me, and she'd sneaked away and back to her room. "Didn't know what he'd do to me if'n he'd caught me there on that bench and come to think I'd heard. Couldn't sleep all night for it," she said. And two days later, when Candice died, she knew Candice had been murdered. "He done killed her," she said. "I know he did, 'cause there wasn't no tow rope."

Remembering the picture on Felicity's cell phone, I asked, "Didn't anybody notice the rope wasn't in the boat?"

"They was all too busy shoutin' and cryin' and gettin' Miss Candice out of the boat onto the dock, 'n I just dropped the rope on the dock to try to help 'cause I couldn't believe at first she was dead."

"And you told nobody, Missy?"

"No, ma'am. Not me. This ol' lady, she was scared right down into her bones. I raised the boy 'n I done knew what he had for a temper. I seed him rise up so violent that he killed things, like that puppy belonged to Mr. Ashley that wouldn't obey, so he strangled it, he did, and some canary birds Felicity kept in a cage that he said woke him up mornings with their singin', so he took them out and drowned them in a bucket full of water right in front of Felicity. They was such pretty little things, and Felicity loved them so. She cried 'n cried after them for days."

There was more, much more. Candice and Freddy had long been good friends. "Them two, they was always together," Missy said. "Almost like sisters, they was, and after that night, when Candice and him was fightin' and he got so mad, Miss Candice and Miss Freddie, they done got thick as fleas. Spent the whole next evenin' together in Miss Freddie's room whisperin' 'n with the door locked."

"Oh?"

"Yes, ma'am. That's the truth."

"Missy, after Candice died and you packed up her things, did you see her iPhone anywhere?"

"Now, how could I do that, when she done give it to Miss Freddie?"

"Her iPhone? Freddie has it? How do you know that?"

"Cause I seed it. Miss Freddie, she had it out on her desk one day, that's how I know. And I seed her puttin' it away in that little safe in her office. That's how."

"And you haven't seen it since."

"Not me, no, ma'am."

Things were coming together, I thought. Felicity's photos were indeed taken the day Candice died and only a few minutes before her death occurred. *Of all the places,* I thought, *to find strong evidence of murder. On the iPhone of a complete innocent.*

I was very aware, however, that I still needed more definite proof of criminality where Congressman Connors was concerned, and hopefully with it a connection to sex trafficking with Asia in order to seal up the case. Murder or no, suspicion of him as a pedophile, no matter how strong, was still just suspicion. But there had to be, nevertheless, a pretty good reason for his former wife's fury with him for taking pictures of some little girl who Missy had told me about and for Freddie hiding away those pictures Candice had put on her cell phone.

I was glad that when I'd been with the New Orleans police, one of the forensic guys had taught me how to crack a safe.

THIRTEEN

The evening of that same day and in spite of Freddie's telling me I'd have great photo ops at the forthcoming foundation picnic, Charlotte made it clear that the family's tolerance of a guest, even though one there to benefit them, was wearing thin. I still had work to do, however, and I immediately contacted the editor of *Great American Families* on the secured twenty-four-hour number I'd been given if I had a serious reporting problem, and asked if she couldn't find a way to get the Warriners to accept my stay for a few more days.

The editor picked up on it at once. I'd hardly finished talking to her when she telephoned Lonsdale Hall and managed to reach Charlotte. It was essential to the story that Miss Henley, her reporter, stay on a few more days, notably to cover the annual A Future for Girls Foundation picnic at Lonsdale Hall that Charlotte would be hosting. It worked. Charlotte, with anger in her eyes, came to my room as I was going to bed to tell me she'd had a rethink and that I'd be more than welcome to stay.

That day was soon enough. The next morning at Lonsdale Hall, preparations by the staff for the annual garden party and picnic hosted by Charlotte began almost before breakfast. By ten o'clock, endless food had been prepared and tables set out for the buffet lunch along with several dozen picnic lunchboxes, and some men had arrived long ahead of time to put up two marquees to shade the guests and the food. The skies were clear and the day turned out to be as promised and typical for the bayou country—humidly hot with a possible thunderstorm at its end.

Around eleven-thirty, the guests began arriving, parking their cars by the dozen along the driveway under the great southern live oaks. To my eye, their occupants looked as wealthy as the cars. There were BMW convertibles and Range Rovers and Cadillacs and a foreign contingent consisting of a Jaguar, a Ferrari, and one exotic car I couldn't identify but guessed it to be a Lamborghini.

Some twenty children who were well-dressed and as healthy looking as possible arrived in three SUVs and were barely able to contain their excitement, while shortly after them a different group appeared in a small and shabby bus with IBERIA PARISH lettered on its side and its windows barred as though it were a prison van. Supervised by several uniformed county welfare matrons, they were a pale and sickly group and had been collected, I learned, from a city orphanage and from various foster homes. Little attention had been paid to their grooming other than a ribbon here and there in the hair of some and new sandals on the feet of those whose feet would have been bare otherwise. They looked bewildered and frightened, and as though to avoid any contact with the well-dressed healthier children, they were given lunchboxes and herded to where there was a trestle table and chairs under a tree well apart from all the rest.

Within minutes and as the adults, both men and women dressed in formal garden party clothes, gathered in groups to drink punch and line a buffet table, the clearly well-off children were running about unrestricted, shrieking and laughing with pleasure, while watched in silence by the underprivileged group at the trestle table.

Once the garden party got going, I set to work and managed to take scores of iPhone pictures of the society women guests as well as the two different groups of girls. Seeing Charlotte tied up, I realized it was a perfect time to get Felicity's phone back and to see if I couldn't also access Candice's iPhone, because Freddie wasn't a problem either. She'd left early that day for her condominium in Baton Rouge. "Can't stand garden parties. If you need anything, Joanne, just give me a call. I've left my number scrawled on a notepad on my desk."

So with Felicity's phone nestled securely in my camera equipment bag and taking a chance on Ashley not appearing yet again, I slipped away from the party and headed for the house. Half way there, I stopped dead. Only a few feet from me was a man I hadn't seen before or photographed, an Englishman by his clothes and his voice when I heard him speak to several people to whom he had attached himself. He was rather flamboyantly dressed but dissolute looking, and he struck me at once as one of those characters you see in an old film on international espionage who has expatriated himself for so long as to almost become one of the natives.

Alarm bells in me went off. An Englishman here? There was an Englishman on my list. One Clarence Hart-Bromley. Could it possibly be? No. It wasn't possible. He's in Malaysia. It had to be someone else. Calm down, Kasie, there are millions of Englishmen all over the world. I took a shot or two of him without his realizing and was about to ask him his name when he suddenly turned away and launched himself at some dowager-type lady and her escort. People swirled around them, and I was cut off.

My alarm bells quieted. I stood there in frustration a moment; I could hardly follow the man about. Then thinking I was just being overanxious—and worse, unprofessional—I got a grip on myself. Letting excitement take the place of quiet judgement isn't wise when on a case, and my job was to report, not pursue. I'd let Gutierrez know tonight, send him the shots I'd taken. If, in a million-to-one chance, the guy was Hart-Bromley, Gutierrez could handle it from there. I continued on into the house, but feeling vaguely neglectful by the time I had gone up the front steps and into the hall—perhaps I should have followed him and got his name? Then, and as I approached the stairs, right in front of me, I saw Miss Davies just as she reached the foot of them. She was clearly in a hurry and was clutching a type sheet.

My bells rang again. Suddenly. And caution fled. I thought fast, almost without actually thinking, and acted even faster. Miss prissy pince-nez was an unexpected gift from heaven. I deliberately blocked her way and she nearly ran headlong into me, letting out a silly, half-stifled shriek of surprise when she stopped just in time.

I made apologetic noises but kept her from going on. "Miss Davies," I said, "would you happen to know the name of the distinguished English gentleman man who is one of the guests?"

Flustered, she managed to rely. "English, English? Oh, yes, I think so …" She glanced at her type sheet, and I saw it was a list of the guests. "Yes," she said. "He is Mr. Clarence Hart-Bromley."

I held down new stabs of excitement; my alarm bells had been right. Muttering "thank you" and some nonsense about "such an interesting man," I ducked past her and went on up the stairs. My head buzzed. The connection the FBI sought with Thailand and Malaysia was right here in the house. But I calmed myself from jumping to any overly quick conclusions. *Was* and at the same time *wasn't.* He was a wanted man, but unofficially as there was no evidence to support his involvement in sex trafficking, only conjecture and suspicion, and I had no way of knowing, let alone proving, what his immediate connection was here at Lonsdale Hall without asking the kind of questions that my being a mere photographer for a magazine didn't warrant and which could give my covert presence away.

I went directly to my room, locked myself in, and sent shots of him and his name with a full encrypted report to Gutierrez. That done, and with a sense of satisfied relief, I went down the hall to

Charlotte's room. I was beginning to feel I was earning my keep. A lot of things were coming together, and Hart-Bromley wasn't the least of them, even though spotting him and nailing a clear identification was mostly luck.

Returning the iPhone to the shoe in the shoe box took only a minute. The job done, I headed for Freddie's office and as a precaution dialed the number Freddie had left with an excuse ready for doing it if she answered. Ridiculous as it seemed, I was beginning to strike *impossible* from my thoughts, and if Freddie for any reason was on to me, her leaving could be a fake and Freddie close by, but I had to chance it. There was no answer. *However,* I thought, *perhaps she was somewhere at lunch.*

The office looked down at the driveway circle in front of the house. Checking to see if Freddie might have unexpectedly come back, I saw no sign of her distinctive bright-red BMW convertible. Closing the office door, I locked it. If Ashley were to try to enter, I could always explain it being locked by my need not to be interrupted while taking difficult overhead pictures from the window of the garden party.

Before going to the safe, however, I embarked on a quick search. If I should find Candice's iPhone,

I was almost certainly going to need a password. Candice was not Felicity. I tried to imagine myself Freddie. Where would she have written it down, because I was certain she probably had. The meticulous neatness of her office indicated a reasonably organized mind. l made my search methodical even though aware constantly of the minutes ticking away. I looked first on the desk, then in it, and to my relief in one drawer I opened, I came across a small notebook in which Freddie, as many people do, had carefully listed a good number of passwords. Among them was one opposite the name Candice. It was "freedom35."

I heaved an enormous mental sigh of relief. *Okay for that,* I thought, *now for you,* and eyed the safe, a short table-height steel mass nestled against some file cases. When I'd packed to come on the job, it had seemed foolishly superfluous, but I had brought it anyway, with the thought *Who knows if…?* With it, I knelt before the safe and, fixing the two ear pieces of the stethoscope, one in each ear, I applied the microphone close to the area of the safe's lock, noting before I spun the dial on the safe's front what number it was on. For all I knew, Freddie had put it on that number when last using the safe so she'd know, if it had changed, that someone had been meddling.

A left safe or a right safe, meaning which way to first turn the dial? It was anybody's guess. I chose, and very slowly and very methodically, I began to turn the dial to the left, twice slowly once around and back to the number, and on a third turn heard an almost inaudible click. Smiling faintly, I began very slowly to turn the dial to the right, back to where I'd started, and then on the second turn I heard another faint click and stopped. *Now, be very careful,* I warned myself, and I began slowly, slowly to turn the dial back to the left. Halfway around to where it had been I heard the third click.

I sat back, took the stethoscope out of my ears and turned the handle of the safe door. With a faint protest from its heavy steel hinges It swung open to reveal a tier of four drawers occupying one half of the interior and three slender vertical filing slots rising from safe's bottom to its top on the other half.

Ignoring the file section, I opened the top drawer and found only odds and ends of jewelry. On the third drawer down, I instantly recognized the rectangular flatness of an iPhone. I took it out, and my nerves jarring as more and more I became aware of time gone by, I took a deep breath, thumbed it on and tried "freedom35." To my utter, almost overwhelming relief, it worked, and I began a search. In less than a minute, I was rewarded with what had been Candice's photo album.

There were scores of pictures. Riffing through them, I went to the window and looked out. There was again no sign of Freddie's car. I resumed my search. More and more photos and still more; another minute of desperate anxiety, and I was finally rewarded—three pictures of little girls together. All, both in their almost threadbare clothing and in their sad personal appearance, had *poverty* and *orphan* written all over them.

A fourth and fifth pictures were of yet another lost-looking little girl and showed her standing in the courtyard of a building identified by a worn letters chiseled into the masonry over its door as PARISH HOME, which I took to be an orphanage. She was about seven or eight, her unwashed hair limp and straggly, her frail little body thin and underfed. In one picture, her unwashed shift, which was all she wore, looked worn nearly to shreds.

In the other picture, in which I could see Lonsdale Hall far in the background, she was naked.

I had transferred the pictures to my iPad when I sensed rather than heard a movement down below in the front hall. I rose sharply and heard Charlotte's voice. There seemed no reason for her to come to Freddie's office, but I remembered that the door had been opened when I'd come in. Charlotte had to go past the office to get to her own, if that was her intent, and she might conceivably wonder why it was shut and try to open it. In seconds, I put the iPhone back in the safe, closed it, twirled the knob around to the number it had been on before I'd opened it, unlocked the office door, and had only just got back to the window with a pretense of shooting pictures of the garden party below with my Canon when I heard Charlotte's masculine voice in the doorway. "Oh, it's you. Did you have Freddie's permission to be in here? She doesn't like anybody in the office."

I put on a broad smile I didn't feel. "I'm sure she wouldn't mind. She said she'd left her phone number for me on her scratch pad in case I needed her, and it turned out to be the ideal place from which to get good overhead shots of your party. I felt that down below I had disturbed your guests enough. People don't like a camera forever in their faces."

She was expressionless in a moment of silence and then said, "Miss Davies tells me you needed to know the name of one of our guests."

I had expected that and was prepared in case at some time she asked. "We have to know the names of any guests whose photograph we publish, Mrs. Warriner. It's legally required, but for the life of me I can't remember now what she said. I didn't have anything with which to write it down. I'll get it again from Miss Davies later." And added boldly, "He was some Englishman, I thought."

Charlotte sniffed and then said, and as though

just to one-up me, "I've told Fredericka often to lock her door." She turned away, but before she disappeared, I noted, her eyes swept the room, resting especially on the desk, to see if anything had been displaced, and I thought how well the *b* word fitted her.

Packing up my things, I knew that given the big woman's surprising unpleasantness that my days there were now most definitely numbered. In fact, that evening with the garden party finally over and the family having a late, light dinner, Charlotte asked pointedly, and regardless of my editor's call to her, how much longer I would be there. "I suppose regretfully that you will be running off now, Joanne. You must have taken thousands of photos, and we've all been interviewed except for dear Connors. What more could you possibly have to do?"

Regretfully, my Great-Aunt Tilly, I thought, but that did it for me, knowing I would have to act quickly if I were to gather what I thought could be final and definitely incriminating information. That meant New Orleans first thing in the morning.

I encrypted my information of the day to Gutierrez and my plans for the morrow, made sure my door was firmly locked, and went to bed, but it was a long time before I could calm my sense of urgency enough to sleep.

But if I felt nervous about what I'd uncovered that day, so did the powers over me at the FBI in Baton Rouge. Turning in for the night himself, Jermyn Gutierrez, checking his laptop and getting my report, immediately put in a call on his secure line to Tom Whitman and read it to him. "Sounds nasty to me," he said. "Should I pull her?"

Tom thought for what seemed forever before he finally answered. "Yeah, it's dicey, but no. I don't think yet. … If we take her out of there and her optimism is justified, we might well blow what's possibly turning into a big a case just as it was resolved. She used to be a cop, and is tough. And she's smart. She's been briefed on what to do, and if they get wise, finally, and come down on her, I think we have to trust in her ability to get *herself* out."

Adding it all up, reappraising me, Jermyn acceded. But he had as much trouble getting to sleep as I did.

FOURTEEN

I drove into town very early in the morning before anybody was up. Erik had begun setting the table for breakfast. I detoured on my way to the front door, and with him towering over me like a giant, asked him to tell the family when they came down that I needed to run proofs of most of the pictures I'd taken to make sure I wouldn't have to do some again. I turned to go, and then turned back and said, "Erik, can I trust your silence about something?"

He looked puzzled and protectively reverted to servility. "Please to do anything I can to help you, ma'am."

I took a breath. Was I taking a chance? I didn't

think so. I had a gut feeling that Erik would never reveal a word I said, and I couldn't stand anymore not lighting some kind of a candle of hope for him and his mother. I looked him straight in the eye and said, "Erik, I am not who I seem to be to the family, or to you. I'm not here just to photograph, I'm here for another reason, and I'm soon to make it certain that your days here, as a virtual slave, your mother's as well, are nearly over. Trust me that I'm right."

I didn't wait for an answer. I rested a reassuring hand on one of his an instant and then quietly left.

Traffic was light and my trip faster than usual. New Orleans was just coming to life when I arrived, and my first stop was the precinct house that for three years had once been home to me. My old partner wasn't there. "He's on vacation," I was coldly told by the desk sergeant, a tough looking young black officer I didn't know. She was seated behind a chest-high barrier that raised her authoritatively up above anyone entering, and she at once defensively assumed an attitude that I thought could spell trouble of some sort.

I was prepared for the disappointment of not seeing my old partner. I had come to New Orleans rather than go direct to FBI headquarters in Baton Rouge because I thought the FBI might not immediately have on hand local police information that I planned to look for. It was a little out of their domain could take up valuable time for them to round it up, and I had virtually run out of time.

I also thought of the nearly impossible chance that I might be followed. By whom I had no idea; the household had been asleep when I left, but I was getting paranoid with the stress I was under, and besides, Gutierrez had told me to stay away unless it was absolutely necessary. "With that crowd," he'd said, "you never know. They'll go to any extent to protect what they're up to and someone other than the family could be shadowing you before you even get to Lonsdale Hall. When you go undercover, dear child," he'd added, showing the paternal concern of a forty-year veteran, "you go under all the way."

I wanted information that required authority, however. I had driven evasive tactics in heavy traffic that were guaranteed to shed any shadower, and I was prepared for the desk sergeant to refuse any request unless I pulled rank. Gutierrez had given me an up-to-date Baton Rouge police identity card saying I had the rank of detective inspector. Since he didn't offer any explanation, I hadn't asked him why not an FBI one. I guessed if there was serious trouble, the FBI didn't what whomever to know that there was a federal investigation on. Knowledge that the FBI was investigating might cause serious retreat into almost impossible obscurity by any criminals on the international scene, while a lesser threat would be seen in the Baton Rouge police.

I had hidden the ID under the inner sole of one of my shoes, and on the way to New Orleans had extracted it. Now I fished it from secondary hiding, a slit in the lining of my shoulder bag, and flashed it. It immediately eliminated an unwelcoming scowl, and I said, "I need a quick check of your missing persons' gallery, if you could manage it."

The desk sergeant came around fast and smiled. "Sure, chief. Not a problem." She turned and shouted back at a tired-looking middle-aged cop in his shirtsleeves who was slouched at a desk staring at a laptop. "Augie?" And then said to me, "You couldn't pull it up at Baton Rouge?"

I smiled back mysteriously and said, "I'm stuck on a job that keeps me here, and my lap's down for the day getting surgery on some guy's bench, so I thought, why not?"

"Sure," the sergeant said. "Come on around." She pressed a button, there was a buzz and a waist-high door swung open in the barrier, admitting me to the area behind it. I went over to Augie's desk, said, "Hi," pulled up a chair next to his, and got out my iPhone. I thumbed up the pictures of the little girl I'd lifted from Candice's cell when I'd retrieved it from Freddie's safe and showed them to him.

Still slouched and not speaking, Augie took a look then punched at his laptop key board a dozen times with one index finger. A file came up and he began to scroll down pictures of missing people.

They were of all types and ages, from senile old men who, an accompanying text said, suffered Alzheimer's and had wandered away, to infants stolen from maternity wards in hospitals.

Well over two dozen had scrolled by when my breath suddenly caught. "Hold it," I said. Augie obeyed, a picture froze, and, leaning forward, close to the screen, while nearly elbowing Augie aside, I compared the photo of the missing girl to the ones on Candice's iPhone. It was unmistakably the same child and said she'd disappeared from a parish orphanage.

"Got it?" came from Augie, trying to straighten up and finally speaking.

"Got it, "I said. I slowly let out my breath. "And how. Thanks so much."

I started to rise when Augie said, "Hold on. I think I remember that one. I think she might have been found. What's it all about?"

"Murder," I said. "Among other things."

"Ah, yes," he muttered. And began again to expertly stab away at his keyboard. His screen convulsed and then came up with a photo file of those the police had been called in on after they'd been killed, murdered, or were suicides, as well as those the police had killed themselves. He began scrolling down endlessly, one picture after another of bodies and heads mutilated by bullets, and I thought, *Jesus, what's gone wrong in this country? Why don't*

they take guns away from everybody like they did in
Australia? It's crazy. We're all living in a blood bath.

And then my breath caught again, and blood
pounded in my ears. Augie stopped at a picture of
a little girl, dead and lying on a police stretcher.
She was naked, and her body looked beaten and
bruised, her hands broken and badly cut. Half of
one leg was missing.

"This is the one, I think," Augie said. "She was
found three years ago floating in the Bayou Teche
a dozen miles south of New Iberia. Croc had been
nibbling on her. Croc or giant snapper. Made the
cops there sick, they said. Poor little thing. Somebody's child. Autopsy said she'd drowned, so she
was still alive when dumped."

He was right. There was no question but that
it was the same little girl as the one in Candice's
pictures, and the one on the missing persons list,
and looking at her on his monitor, I felt sick myself.
I'd seen another little girl just like her years before,
but not in a photograph. She'd been in reality. My
years with the New Orleans force had toughened
me against death, but this in my life again? When
I took a picture with my iPhone, my hands shook
and my mouth felt too dry for speech.

Leaving the police precinct, I was in a state of
near numbing shock. "Step one," I said to myself.
"You've tied the photo on Candice's iPhone of a
sad little orphan girl, one Candice had taken from

Connors's iPhone, to a horrifyingly brutal murder. Now for step two."

That meant more proof. What I had so far could be denied as purely circumstantial. The child could have been murdered by anybody, and not necessarily by Connors, nor at Lonsdale Hall.

The day was perilously hot. New Orleans sweltered. I took time to park by a Dunkin' Donuts, and with an excuse to cool off in the air-conditioning, went in, made an important phone call, leaving a message for an old friend with his assistant when he was busy, and drank a Pepsi. After pulling myself together, I went on to the next stop; that was a CVS Pharmacy and where at their photo counter I had the photo I'd taken of the iron shackle in the slave jail at Lonsdale Hall made into a glossy five-by-seven. Tucking the glossy into my shoulder bag, I then headed for step two.

Of the several coroner's offices in New Orleans, the one sandwiched between the French Quarter and Louis Armstrong Park that I drew up before in my battered Toyota was perhaps the least likely to win an architectural award. Its long, squat ugliness, its windows as though merely painted rectangles stamped onto its flat concrete surface and unadorned by any cornice or design, shouted dull municipal bureaucracy. Only the presence of several ambulances and police cars parked on the broad treeless expanse before it indicated life in a building dedicated to death.

Showing my police identity at the guard's desk in the soulless lobby and registering the fact that I had an appointment to see Dr. Simon Alastair, I was announced to his office and took myself up an undecorated flight of stairs to an equally barren corridor that led past several offices to one of the laboratories. Giving its door a quick knock, I entered a relatively small and cluttered place of lab tables, microscopes, phials, and medical trays with shelves arrayed with bottles, many containing body parts floating in formaldehyde. There were several technicians at work, and as I entered, a young Asiatic woman, half her face masked and wearing surgical gloves, turned from putting away some slides. "Can I help?"

I said, "I'm here to see Dr. Alastair. I called. I'm Kasie Sanders." And suddenly realized that I'd used my own name when I'd become accustomed to being called Joanne. It made me smile inwardly but warned me yet again not to make the same slip back at Lonsdale Hall.

"Oh, yes. I gave Alastair your message, and he's expecting you, but I'm afraid he was just called down the hall to refrigeration to supervise two students in an autopsy. I can take you there if you wouldn't mind. There's one on a table at the moment and not very pretty, I'm afraid. Whoever it was, he was messed up in a shootout."

"Par for the course," I said and managed a casual smile. I hated morgues. The still, cold air and silence in them always had seemed to me as dead as the corpses that were finding a temporary resting place on trays slid into freezing degree compartments lining a wall and brought out to lie stiffly and anonymously on a stretcher for autopsy or identification—lives, where most of them were concerned, that meant nothing to anybody.

I said, "I don't mind. I've had plenty of morgue experience."

"I'm Sally," the young woman said. She stripped off her mask revealing a cheerful face and then, dumping her surgical gloves, led the way after we shook hands.

Simon Alastair's big horn-rims and shaggy dark hair, that almost looked like a wig for a theatrical, belied his age. He wasn't twenty-four; he was more than double that. He was watching two young pathology students who, gowned and wearing face masks, were drilling into the smashed skull of a naked corpse, and as I followed Sally into the refrigeration room, he was saying, "When you drill the fourth hole, making a square, you can then use your saw from hole to hole and suction-lift out the entire bone plate to give you far greater space to work in. Helps you to relax and go whole hog with a lot of head traumas." He looked across the corpse and saw Sally and then me, and a look of delight spread over his features.

"Good Heavens! Kasie Sanders! Sally said Kasie, and she was right. Couldn't believe my ears." He was a big guy and came quickly around the autopsy table to give me an almost crushing bear hug. "What a wonderful surprise. Downstairs they said you were with the Baton Rouge force, and I couldn't quite make sense of that. Should I not broadcast possible subterfuge?"

"If you can possibly not," I said. "And sorry, I've got the cuffs on against saying more. At least at this moment, anyway."

"So don't, dear child. You're talking to a fellow coconspirator against the evil that surrounds us all. I'll consider my all-consuming curiosity no longer a candidate for autopsy on a secret." He turned to a smiling Sally and added, "Kasie and I are old friends. Back in her investigative days, she was my favorite cop. She brought in two or three of my most interesting cases." He solemnly slalomed me then casually sat on the autopsy table, nudging the corpse over to give himself room and saying, "Here, you, don't be a hog." And then to me, "So what brings you here? I can't believe it's my legendary charm."

I laughed, and took a crossed-fingers breath,

and said, "Simon, I need a big, big favor from you."

"Giant size? Do you, now? You come around after disappearing for four years and expect favors? And here I thought it was unrequited love." He grinned. "Well, okay, then. For you, anything. Especially when it's clearly the clandestine and covert, so let's get away from Mr. X here and go have a sit in my office and reveal. Sally, be an angel and whip us up a couple of javas, please, for me and my secret visitor here whom you never, ever laid eyes on today, yes?"

Sally smiled agreement and disappeared, and, with a casual "Carry on, guys," to the two autopsy novices, and an arm around me, my old friend escorted me out of the refrigeration room, with its ongoing autopsy, and down the soulless corridor to his small cluttered office. There, unceremoniously shoving a pile of papers and a tote bag off a chair across from a beat-up, hopelessly cluttered desk, he bade me sit and be comfortable. Nothing then would do but that I bring him up to date on every moment of my life since I'd resigned from the New Orleans police until Jermyn Gutierrez got hold of me. I stopped just short of that when I came to the end of describing my last wedding reception and, in an abrupt silence, he simply stared at me, expressionless, until finally he said, "That's it?"

"That's it," I said.

"You leave me as you photograph carousing

wedding guests and sneak a plate of wedding cake. Then blank. Fair enough. So on to business. What is this willing service my once favorite cop has come to ask from me?"

I said, "Two things, Simon. Both forensic and both may be real toughies."

Simon said, "Shoot," and then, resting his arms on one of the paper piles that cluttered the desk's surface, he leaned forward, all ears. "And …?"

"*And* is this," I said and took the little plastic bag from my shoulder bag with the tissue I'd wiped across the iron cuff in the slave jail at Lonsdale Hall when I'd gone there with Felicity. "I need a DNA match with a corpse that was either here or possibly in the morgue in New Iberia or at Baton Rouge three years ago, which you might conceivably be able to quickly bully out of a colleague. I showed him the picture I'd taken from Augie's laptop. "This child. A little girl found trussed up and floating in the Bayou Teche."

"Oh, dear. That one?" Simon looked shocked and surprised me with, "Yes, we did have her here, actually. She was due at Baton Rouge, but their morgue, like half the morgues in the country, was filled up solid with the veritable avalanche of ODs our narco nation is bedeviled by, and they shipped her to us. Perfectly awful case. But, Kasie, she's been cremated."

"You did a DNA wipe first?"

"Of course. It's in our database, too, but it might take a little time to bring it up. Our system is temporarily down."

I tossed him the plastic bag, and he said, "What's the other thing?"

I reached deep into my shoulder bag again and fished out the glossy photo of the shackle I'd had printed at CVS and scaled it at him over the desk's debris. "Take a look at this. There's a possible blood stain or dried blood on it. If it is blood, is there any possible way of determining the type?"

He let out a low whistle. "I dunno. That's a toughie, all right. Modern science is great, but blood type from a photo? If it is indeed blood, I might have to send it away. That identification would require a color spectrum coding we don't have here. There's one in a private lab in Cincinnati run by a crazy scientist type I know, or possibly at a lab in Canada, that might come up with an answer."

"I'd settle for it just being blood for the time being."

"Let's have a look, then."

Simon pulled a heavy magnifying glass from a drawer in his desk and applied it to the photo. "Yeah," he said after a moment. "That's blood, all right. Stake my job on it. Do you want me to send it off?"

"Yes. Please." I wrote down my personal email. Just a one-letter message. A, B, or O, okay? And the

DNA. Just match or no match."

"With the database number for the one in the photo? Gotcha. No charge."

We spent a pleasant few minutes then, reminiscing. I heard all about his latest child and his wife's job with an astronomy group. "She's starstruck," he said, laughing. Used to be Brad Pitt, now it's Orion or one of his gang up there in the firmament. And then said, "Got to get you married, Kasie."

"Find me someone," I said, hiding the instant pain I felt whenever anyone said that to me, and the older I get, the more they do. When I left him, it lingered, and along with it a sense of being in a time warp where nothing would ever happen in my personal life to make it any different than what it was.

FIFTEEN

Every police detective knows that sometimes you get a lucky break in a case. Sometimes something occurs that comes at you completely and unexpectedly out of the blue and can make or break a case. That happened to me within minutes after I left Simon and the morgue.

I rarely take the main route out of town. To avoid heavy traffic, I usually stick to mostly untraveled back streets. I was headed along a narrow French Quarter one-way that wove a tortured path between crowded old buildings with their wrought-iron balconies when I found myself, perversely, in just that—in a line of cars blocked to a standstill by a UPS truck making a delivery. I was virtually at an intersection where a small side street, almost an alley, crossed the one I was on, and taking my eyes from the unmoving car immediately in front of me, I happened to glance at a restaurant I was directly opposite. When I did, I got a shock.

Of all people, I saw, standing outside it, Freddie Mayworth. With her was a tall, fashionably dressed woman whom I quickly recognized from old police files. It was Amelie Faure. Then, even as I sat frozen behind my steering wheel and staring in numbed disbelief, the UPS truck pulled away, the car behind me honked for me to "get moving," and the two women went together into the restaurant.

There were moments in my life when what I did seemed disconnected from thought or planning, like when I'd blocked Miss Davies in the hall to get the Englishman's name. Looking back, this was one of them. Without thinking, I reacted. I swung the Toyota down the side street and then, looking frantically for a place to park and seeing none, found a gap and drove right up on the narrow sidewalk to stop within a few feet of the restaurant's kitchen door with a pedestrian, whom I'd nearly hit, shouting at me. If I was ticketed, I was the law, I thought.

Elbowing past a surprised kitchen worker lounging in the doorway and who came to life too late to protest, I found myself in the back of the steamy hot kitchen, where cooks, chopping and mixing food ingredients in bowls and tending simmering pots and pans on two large stoves, stopped work and gawked at my unexpected presence. I grabbed one wearing a chef's hat who seemed authoritative and said, "Quick! Where's the boss?"

The man flushed angrily. "I'm the boss. Who the hell are you?"

I hadn't reconcealed my police ID. Pulling it from my shoulder bag I shoved it up to his face to read. Then, not waiting for him to speak or even react and while he still stared at it, I snapped an order. "Keep giving me a hard time to yourself, okay? This is an urgent police matter."

As a cop I had learned that if you jump on someone fast enough and order them really tough, they mostly obey like automatons. Still not waiting for him to speak, I quickly pulled my Canon camera from my shoulder bag, triggered it to record, and thrust it into his hands. "Here! Take this and put it on any unoccupied back table. Don't let anyone see you do it, don't let anyone sit there, and don't let any of your staff touch it."

I pushed him commandingly toward the double swing doors through which a waiter was just coming with a tray load of dishes. "Go. Right now, quick time, or you'll be in big trouble. No, it's not a fucking bomb, and don't argue or ask questions."

To my relief, and after staring a moment and seeming to think, he turned away from me, and I watched him go through the double doors with my

Canon. When they'd closed behind him, I peered through the small head-high glass window in one, and watching, saw him put the camera on an empty table close by.

The restaurant was relatively long and narrow. It was now well past lunch hour, and there were only a handful of customers who still lingered over coffee. I could see Freddie and Amelie Faure as they seated themselves at a table near the front door where two men were already seated. At a distance and in the restaurant's soft low-key light, it was difficult to see faces, but I was almost certain one was Asiatic. The other I recognized immediately. It was Clarence Hart-Bromley.

The restaurant owner-chef came back, and I said to him in a now less commanding tone. "Okay, thank you. I'll be back here after that foursome upfront leaves. And keep buttoned up, okay? Got it?"

He said, "Not a problem," and back outside I found more than one irate pedestrian gathered at my car where a traffic cop was writing out a ticket. When I identified myself as the owner and he was checking Gutierrez phony driver's license in the name of Joanne Henley, a surprised and slightly puzzled look swept his face. "Hey, aren't you? Yeah you were...."

He didn't finish. The owner-chef had appeared in the kitchen doorway behind us, and I cut the cop off fast with my identification, bringing a broad grin to his face. "I'll be damned. I wondered what had happened to you."

"Afraid telling you all will have to wait," I said quickly. "I'm working and due elsewhere, but fast."

He laughed. "Get the hell out of here, then, before the lieutenant comes by and sees I don't have the cuffs on you."

I got my Toyota off the sidewalk and back down on the street and found a place to park a few blocks away, and sat and waited an hour, the longest hour, I think, I've ever spent anywhere at any time. I was staggered at what I'd run into and kept trying to add things up, to come to grips with the fact that the person whom I'd always had the least suspicion of amidst all the viciousness of the totally suspect Warriner family was more vicious than all of them put together. Looking for Connors Warriner Junior being a pedophile, I'd turned up a rat's nest of what I was sure had to be major sex-trafficking. I felt as though I was sitting on a bomb about to explode and it took a while for me to pull myself together.

When I hiked back to the restaurant and retrieved my camera from the owner, he was his usual grudging self. "Officer, can you tell me what the hell this was all about?"

And I thought, *If only I could.* I felt suddenly so alone, overwhelmed with what I knew and with wanting to share it with someone, with anyone, so as not to have to carry it all by myself for one minute longer. "You can read about it in the papers," I said, "and if you talk about it before then, you'll find yourself explaining why to a judge."

I left him, wondering. And myself innocent that the horror of what I'd learned was just the beginning.

Then something happened that I didn't know about, and it was bad. When you go undercover, you don't take chances. And I had.

After I'd come back and retrieved the camera and was gone, the restaurant owner took his afternoon break before starting to get ready for the dinner crowd. He made himself a coffee and went and sat at the table on which he'd placed the Canon and apparently thought, *Why a camera when it was too dark really for pictures, even if it was a top of the line one? And how did a camera take pictures all by itself? And if it did, wouldn't its flash have told people they were being photographed?*

He'd circled the table a couple of times when I was parked nearby, waiting, and hadn't seen any flashbulb light or heard any clicks or whirring noise that would have indicated the camera was on a timer of some sort. Giving in to temptation when Freddie Mayworth, Amelie Faure, and the two men had gone, he'd finally picked the camera up and examined it. He didn't profess to know much about photography, but he couldn't see anything about the Canon that looked in any way suspicious.

His afternoon break over and going back to the kitchen to start preparing for the dinner crowd, he forgot about it until he closed down for the night and was on his way home to his one-room apartment only a short distance away. Then he remembered and started puzzling again. Somehow, he was sure, the camera had something to do with Amelie Faure, or maybe with the men she was meeting. They were the only foursome. He didn't like the looks of either the bloody chink or the nose-in-the-air limey, but who was he to say about who Amelie associated with. They looked rich enough to pay for girls every night of the week.

He'd got to know Amelie Faure, he catered expensive parties she often gave, and he always treated her girls with drinks and lunches when any of them came in. It was good for a free ride sometimes for him from one particular blond who knew every trick in the books, and Amelie had put in a word with one of her big politician clients when the parish health guys were going to have his license suspended about conditions in his kitchen they said were substandard.

Maybe this was his chance to repay Amelie. If his blond number came in that evening, he'd get her

to slip Amelie a note saying the police had been in
while she was having lunch and had made him do
something real crazy—put a big camera on a back
table until she and the two guys and the lady she
was huddled with had gone.

Or better still, he'd give Amelie a call himself.

SIXTEEN

On the long drive back to Lonsdale Hall from New Orleans, I felt I would have given almost anything not to be returning to the old planation home, beautiful though it was. But I had to. I'd left a lot of camera equipment there, along with personal belongings. I felt willing to abandon all that, but not to appear and say good-bye, while if not possibly blowing my cover, would at least look peculiar enough to cause someone (Freddie? Charlotte?) to call the editor of *Great American Families* to ask questions which could prove embarrassing, or even perhaps cause trouble, not just for her but eventually also for Jermyn Gutierrez.

Thinking over the week I'd spent at Lonsdale

Hall, and for a moment separating from it my feelings about what I'd just learned in New Orleans—the dull, awful horror of that—I saw almost every day I'd spent there as depressing. Added to the overbearing personality of any one of the Warriners, save for Missy and Felicity, was their detestable racism and their clinging so proudly, along with how many countless, far-flung others, to their ancestors' role in the utter horror of the Civil War. In the most beautiful and idyllic surroundings, the atmosphere at Lonsdale Hall was a nightmare of deceitful hypocrisy.

Worse, I was returning to a home and family where, as though the vicious racism and far right ideology of the socially correct Warriners was not enough, the head of the family and a U.S. Congressman was unquestionably a murderer, blackmailed into being one by a wife who held over his head, like the worst kind of Damoclean sword, his sickening guilt of pedophilia.

I had not a single doubt the DNA test would prove that the blood on the shackle in the slave jail I'd visited with Felicity might belonged to the tragic little orphan girl whose life had come to such a bitter end. And I felt my blood run cold when I asked myself the question, how many other little girls like her had met the same fate? The little girl I'd seen as a cop and the child in the photograph I'd lifted from Candice's iPhone were surely not rare or isolated cases. I thought of the pathetic little girls who'd been brought to the annual foundation picnic in the shabby Iberia Parish bus to be kept apart from the healthier children running about wildly and my heart sank. A Future for Girls Foundation was only in its third year, created soon after Candice died and Charlotte was free to do as she wished. Had it been created solely to display children for Connors to see and choose for later abuse, or for other sick sex perverts as well? Reb Bannerman had been at this year's picnic. And how about Hart-Bromley?

Given what I had learned of Charlotte in the brief time I'd been at Lonsdale Hall, I thought the answer was probably yes. And I thought that the only reason no child had been seized at the Foundation garden party this year was probably because of my presence.

I felt as though I was returning to a sewer.

The moment I was clear of New Orleans, I pulled into the parking lot of a mall and switched the Canon camera to Play and listened. In my haste to get it placed and with the added urgency not to be caught at it, I had ordered it put on a table a little out of the maximum range for which it had been calibrated. The recording made, however, clearly indicated that every hideous thing I suspected was true.

It had caught some of the conversation, but not all, and what it had caught was frequently over-ridden by street noises or by the clatter of dishes being served and eaten. But I heard enough and was sure that Forensic, with especially sensitive listening devices, would hear more. I'd had the luck to gather conclusive evidence sought by the FBI of American participation in an international illicit sex-slavery ring.

With no little shock, I realized the probable role played by the small dog cages hanging in the slave jail when the talk between Freddie, Amelie, the Asians, and Hart-Bromley, as they calmly lunched, turned mostly to supply and shipping. It was as though orphaned children being sent out of the States were consumer products, with Hart-Brom-ley blithely saying they could easily market more than they were getting, and with Freddie protesting that the woman who was her source in providing them was limited by the need of extreme caution.

The woman had enlisted an accountant, she said, over whom she had enough to buy his silence, and he constantly adjusted records at the orphan-age, of which the woman was a patron, to hide their disappearance. Each child was listed as being adopted, and extensive adoption records with fic-titious parents were created to deceive state and parish welfare authorities with the occasional suspicion mollified with a substantial bribe. Although the name of the woman wasn't mentioned, who else could it be, I thought, but Charlotte Warriner?

To escape the ever vigilant U.S. immigration authorities, those children who had satisfied the hideous lust of Connors and others were packed two to a cage in the slave jail and smuggled out of the States by way of the Bayou Teche on Connors Chris-Craft to an obscure part of the delta. From there, it was by boat across the Gulf to a Central American country where virtually no questions were ever asked, when they were put on the long flight to hell in Malaysia or Thailand. Shipping was effectively managed by fake passports and tourist visas provided by the Asians, which matched those of women arranged as the children's escorts who, to avoid death by domestic violence or gang warfare at home, were easily recruited as mules.

Price was discussed, and I heard amounts being paid by some utterly venal business men and corrupt politicians that seemed to equal that of luxury cars, as most of the children shipped were kept as sex slaves for many months, even years, only to be dumped to earn their way in the streets when no longer interesting because they had fully matured.

Amelie got a percentage, with a guarantee from her to Freddie of the names of well-known state politicians and businessmen using her service that

Freddie could blackmail when necessary in her business dealings.

Freddie also held a constant threat over Charlotte through her knowledge of Connors's murder of Candice and, once Charlotte was involved in providing children for sex, the big woman's additional fear of losing her coveted social position as a Warriner along with the Warriner millions. The threat guaranteed Freddie her own safely commanding role in the trafficking.

I wasn't taking chances with the camera. Its evidence was too valuable. So was my cell, in which I had a lot of substantiating evidence. The Baton Rouge airport was on my way, and I pulled in to it, parked, and stowed both in a locker where they would be safe until I picked them up in the morning. I crypto-emailed Gutierrez the locker number and tucked away the key with my sunglasses in an eyeglass case in the glove compartment of my Toyota, got out of the parking lot and back onto the highway, and drove on, completely innocent of the effect my email had at the FBI.

When Tom Whitman read my report, he was decisive. "Pull her," he said. "And right now. I don't like it. Amelie Faure hangs out at that restaurant, and the guy who owns it is a first-class bastard.

With what Kasie's run up against there, she could be in way over her head."

Jermyn Gutierrez tried, but my cell rang uselessly in the airport locker.

Traffic was heavy, and what I had learned made it hard for me to keep my mind on driving. My thoughts were in such a whirl over all the final revelations during the course of that day that I missed an exit on the thruway. I had to double back, and then I took two wrong turns on local roads that I knew well.

But even though totally distracted, I felt at the same time an odd sense of relief, and tried to think positively. It was all over and finally out of my hands. I'd done what I'd been assigned to do and got what the FBI wanted. Perhaps, as Gutierrez had hinted, it might lead to a full-time job with them.

Vacation time was looming, too, and I'd arranged a trip back home to Arkansas to see my parents and little sister, who was getting married. The thought of their normalcy and gracious decency in life was an antidote, in part, to all I'd experienced at Lonsdale Hall.

Tonight I would politely say good-bye to all of them there, give Felicity an especially warm hug, and shed being Joanna Henley when I left very early in the morning, with their supposing that I was in for a very long drive back to Baltimore. I was thinking just that as I turned into the long tree-shaded driveway leading up to Lonsdale Hall itself when, in glancing at my rear-view mirror, I saw Freddie's BMW convertible right behind me.

SEVENTEEN

Something inside me froze. Any good resolutions vanished. I told myself, "Don't panic, you know about them, but they don't know about you."

So I drove up the long graveled driveway beneath the towering cover of the great old southern live oaks and parked, taking my time to do so, then got out with no semblance of hurrying, and when Freddie pulled up, I put on a cheerful smile I hardly felt. "Hi. Pleasant coincidence."

Freddie was as good an actress as I. She greeted me back with a friendly smile. We all walked up to the front door together, and Freddie said, "Did you get the photo proofs you said you wanted to check on?"

And I said, "Everything turned out fine. No further work in view." And added, "I feel so sad I have to leave you, but my editor is screaming at me for taking so long."

"You're not going to try to drive tonight, are you? It's a long ways, to say the least."

"No, I won't. But I'll be going at the crack of dawn."

In fact, I had no intention of spending the night. The thought of sleeping there again even for one moment was anathema. Any motel an hour away would have been better if I actually were driving to Baltimore. But I wasn't making that long drive. In an hour I'd be in my own bed in the apartment I shared with Alysia. My intention was to put my personal belongings that evening into my old Toyota for a pretended early start and be on my way without a word to anyone the moment the house was asleep.

"We'll all be sad to see you go," Freddie, said. Which meant to me that of course they wouldn't be. They could get on with their hideous trafficking without the worry of having a stranger in their midst. Ever since I'd discovered what they were up to with the famous Lonsdale Hall and the Warriner name as a front, I'd wondered why they'd ever agreed in the first place to have me down to photograph and interview. I could only think that Charlotte's desire for social prominence took precedence over fear of revelation of her involvement in murder and trafficking in children for sex, and that Freddie had seen my coming as an additional disguising front for it. A major article in *Great American Families* was the most perfect disguise. It would help dispel suspicion if any should ever crop up. Both women had been certain they were entirely safe. How could a little photographer ever breech their wall of carefully planned security?

Charlotte appeared in the hall as we entered, and if she knew as little about me as I innocently thought Freddie did, I had no problem with her. She wore her usual disapproving and disdainfully patronizing look, which I think had settled in permanently on her heavy unfeminine face and to which I'd become thoroughly accustomed.

"Joanne's leaving us first thing in the morning," Freddie told her. "She's decided to stay the night and not attempt brutal night driving."

"I'll pack up things tonight, though," I said. "I don't want to waken anybody doing it tomorrow."

That went well with Charlotte, I could plainly see, but with her usual appalling lack of manners with anyone she considered beneath her or, in my case a traitor to their class, she said not a word to me and had turned away when Freddie said, "Charlotte, If you've got a moment, I'd like to discuss something with you."

Charlotte for an instant looked taken aback but then said, "Of course."

Freddie said. "Good. It won't take long. Just give me a minute to freshen up. I'll be in my office."

I went to my room, packed up my things, and then in about a half hour suffered a last dinner with the family. Connors Warriner Senior was his usual wilted cauliflower self, slumped in his chair, food spooned to him by Erik dribbling down his chin onto his chest. His congressman son was his usual inscrutable silent self. Making no bones at being sociable, he read state papers, a stack of which he'd brought to the table, while he ate. Charlotte, like her husband, said nothing, and Felicity, as usual, wore the slightly anxious look that bordered on frightened whenever she was with them. I kept thinking, *Poor Felicity. She's going to miss me. In all the time I've been here, I'm the only person except for Missy that she's had the nerve to speak to.*

It was left to Freddie to make small talk, which consisted mainly with asking me what route I would take north and how soon the article on the Warriner family would be published. I promised her that most likely it would appear within three months. "I think that's what they have planned," I said. To avoid any possible lawsuit for nonperformance if by any chance my undercover operation had not been successful, the editor of *Great American Families* had indeed planned to use all the pictures I'd taken, plus my interviews and any additional information I could add, for a full-blown article.

After dinner and when it came to saying goodbye, Connors had disappeared without a word, Charlotte managed, barely, a "Thank you for coming," and it was again left to Freddie to be pleasantly polite, to thank me profusely for having come, to invite me to drop in again any time, to call her if in doing the article I found I needed more information, and to have a safe drive home.

When it came to Felicity, I reminded her she'd promised to let me have one of her watercolors and told her she could leave one on the hall table. "And please don't forget to sign it," I said, giving her a hug.

I did as I'd said and quite openly stowed my stuff in the Toyota, and then stayed in my room for what seemed forever, waiting for the silence of sleep to fall over Lonsdale Hall. It was close to midnight when it finally did. I checked to make sure I'd left nothing behind and very quietly went downstairs. I looked on the hall table for the promised watercolor from Felicity and didn't see any, so I continued on and out the front door, closing it behind me as silently as possible.

The sky had clouded over, and the night was pitch dark. I managed to carefully reach my parked Toyota without tripping and falling although once was close to it. I got in, and without turning on the lights yet, was about to start it up when I was thoroughly startled by a knock on my driver's window. My first thought was that it was one of the gardeners, and then I felt a stab of fear. But suppose it wasn't. A second thought flitted of some strange man who could be dangerous. I had a flashlight with me and thinking, *Oh, damn,* and that I was going to be stopped in leaving secretly, I spun it around, and its light flared on the person who had knocked.

It was Felicity. She was in her night dress and robe and looked shaken and frightened.

I rolled my window down and whispered, "Felicity, what's happened? What's wrong?"

"Nothing."

"Nonsense. Tell me." I began hoping desperately that no one would hear us. Waking the family and explaining that I'd changed plans and would drive at night after all was the last thing I wanted.

I flicked off the flashlight, and in the dark I could sense Felicity fidgeting. There was silence and then she burst out. "You have to help me get it."

"Get what?"

"Your present." And as I tried to figure out what she was getting at, she said, "The picture I painted for you."

"Oh, Felicity, that's so sweet. You shouldn't have bothered. Where is it?"

"Charlotte said she was going to take it away, and my paints, too."

"But why didn't you give it to me earlier?"

"I was waiting here for you."

None of it made sense. Feelings of sympathy got the better of me. I quietly got out of the car. And put an arm around her shoulder. "Felicity, what's happened? Why are you out here at this hour?"

"I hid it in the boathouse."

Oh, my God, I thought. I didn't need this. Still whispering, I said, "Can you get it for me? Or better still, why not just tell me where you hid it."

"You couldn't ever find it."

I thought to myself, there are moments when you simply have to act. Hopefully the house was fully asleep and no one had heard us, but I couldn't afford to stand by my car forever. Clearly Felicity was frightened to go to the boathouse on her own. Impulsively, I grabbed her hand. "Come on, then Felicity, and let's be quick," and pulled her toward the path leading through the gardens and then on across the corner of the field.

We went quickly in spite of the darkness. I didn't dare turn on my flashlight until I was certain we were screened by the hedge of lilacs between the driveway and the garden and that no light could be seen either from an upstairs window or over the top of the hedge or through a gap in it. And Felicity wasn't any help. She dragged back on my hand as though reluctant to go to the boathouse at all. *How frightened can you be of a place,* I thought. It wasn't as though she'd never been there before.

The thought should have warned me, even if Felicity's strange behavior didn't, but I had let my heart dominate my head. We reached the boathouse and I said, "Now, show me where, Felicity," and opened the door on the pitch-black interior. I let go of her hand a moment and stepped inside. Felicity didn't answer. "Felicity?"

I'd barely said her name and had half turned to shine my flashlight on her when I was blinded by a sudden flare of bright light that pierced right into my eyes, and at the same time sensed a rushing movement behind me. I felt a stab of fear and then nothing.

EIGHTEEN

To this day, I can't remember coming to the way they do in the movies; a moment or two of sizing it all up and then upright, vague and dizzy for a few minutes but more or less with it and back into action.

It wasn't like that at all. Everything was total confused unawareness, and my entire head a terrible migraine. And then, very slowly, as more and more awareness crept in, I felt sharp pain in my wrists. Why? Where was I?

Bit by bit, and after what seemed a lifetime, I began to be conscious that I was seated with both my arms raised above my shoulders and I couldn't move them. I thought I was in bed and couldn't understand why my arms would be that way. Or was I in my Toyota? Had I had an accident? Was I in a hospital?

The pain in my wrists got worse and spread. My back was agony, and then my legs felt cramps seize them. They were doubled under me somehow. That made me begin to focus, and a blurry nothing slowly became gloomy half-light on a wall beyond me, and in it an open door. It didn't make sense. A wall and a door? Where was I?

And then finally it did make sense as I began to recognize that I was in the slave jail at Lonsdale Hall.

I tried to move and couldn't. My arms held me, and with a sudden wave of terror I began to realize that I was kneeling and shackled to the wall.

It didn't seem real. Why was I there? Faint memories came of Felicity and her knocking on my car window and telling me she had a present. I couldn't remember anything else.

I felt desperately sick, and I think I fainted for a while because suddenly there was a blazing light in my eyes again, and I heard a voice.

"Joanne!" And then, "But you're not Joanne, are you. You're probably somebody else, and you're a bloody cop. Wake up."

My face was slapped hard, several times, jarring my migraine to life with merciless knives. "Wake up, you rotten little bitch. Wake up. What did you do with the camera? Your Canon. Where is it?"

I was slapped again. "Now! Right now! What did you do with it? You've hidden it someplace, haven't you? Where?"

And I finally recognized the voice. It was Fredericka Mayworth. She held a key close to my eyes, and I dimly remembered it was for the airport locker where I'd stowed the Canon and that I'd put it with my sunglasses in the glove compartment of my Toyota. I had a numb frightened regret I hadn't bothered to hide it. "I found this. It's for a locker someplace, yes? You've put it in a locker. Where?" I was slapped again. Hard. "Talk, damn you. Tell me. Where is it?"

When I didn't answer, she tangled a hand in my hair and banged my head hard back into the wall, once, twice and then, yanking my head up, slapped me some more, hard, demanding over and over I tell here where I'd put the Canon, until finally she gave up. "All right, you stupid cop. Keep it to yourself. But you won't for long, I promise you." Her voice was icy with hate and anger. "You're going for a boat ride down the Bayou to a place on the delta where I have friends who will soon find out where it is."

When the light turned away from my eyes for a moment and pointed toward the big doors at the end of the building, I saw her shadowy form holding it, and in the light's glaring beam what I realized was Connors's Chris-Craft, loosely moored to the building.

Freddie turned away from me and muttered over her shoulder, "Give me a hand with her," and I saw and recognized Charlotte in the gloom behind her. She was carrying a shotgun. Even as I registered this and she stepped toward me, something happened unexpectedly and very quickly.

Charlotte let out a screech and seemed to slam down on her side. A giant form loomed, and seizing Freddie by the neck, lifted her clear up into the gloom and smashed her to the dirt next to Charlotte. Her light spun away someplace, its beam shining uselessly on nothing but making enough light for me to let me see who was kneeling beside me. And with a dull sense of bewildered astonishment, I recognized Erik.

I felt his big hands try to loosen the cuff on one of my wrists, heard his voice, "Hang on, lady, hang on," his fumbling to release the bolt that held them. He couldn't, and, frustrated, he literally yanked the entire shackle with its chain from the wall.

Charlotte had risen. She had the shotgun up, but Erik had turned from me and saw her in time. He spun and yanked the gun away from her and swung it. It crushed sickeningly against her head, flying from his grip but sending her down in a huddled silent heap.

As he bent for it, Freddie, up on her knees and closer, scrabbled and got it first and swung it around on him, but she was too late. Something in me had come alive. Without thinking, even without realizing it was me doing it, only that I had to bring her down, only that, I swung my free arm, still shackled but free now, and the heavy iron plate that had fixed the shackle to the wall crashed hard across her head.

And with the same free hand, I groped frantically at my hip until I found the Band-Aid there and the faint lump beneath it, and pressed it three times.

NINETEEN

Poor Felicity. They had forced her to entice me to the boathouse, first with loving smiles—they had a wonderful surprise for me, they'd told her, a thank-you gift for all I had done to put them in *Great American Families.*

Then, when she'd balked, the threat. It was do it or else, and she'd had no idea why, only that she had to because if she didn't, they told her, they would take her paints away forever: paints, easel, paper to paint on, everything. In short, the world she lived in and her life.

When Charlotte, with a heavy belaying pin, had felled me, Felicity fled in terror, choked with guilt at the part she'd played. Wandering, distraught, she'd childlike gone to Missy and babbled out what had happened, and a badly frightened Missy, certain of something terrible, had woken Erik, and Erik, remembering and believing in what I had said to him and fearful all chances for him and his mother might be gone, had frantically rushed to the boathouse.

Finding the Chris-Craft missing, he was about to give up when Missy, who'd come with him, noticed the track of crushed grass where I'd been dragged across the field by Charlotte and Freddie, and he followed it to the slave jail, where I was to be kept until I regained my senses and gave up where I'd hidden the Canon.

It all seems so long ago now, like the very worst sort of horrible dream, and yet it was only last year around this same time. What was recorded on the camera, along with forensic evidence Simon Alastair successfully collected, put both Freddie and Charlotte in jail, where they are still awaiting trial for abducting young girls and sending them out of the country for sex slavery. Clarence Hart-Bromley was stopped and arrested as he was boarding a plane to fly back to Malaysia, and later extradited, now faces their form of justice.

The FBI forced from Freddie the location of a safe house in the delta where they had planned to take me before they dumped me dead into the wilds of some delta swamp to be found, if ever, decomposed beyond recognition. They were too late to get the Asiatic who awaited me. Realizing that something might have gone wrong, when Freddie didn't show up on time, he had fled, and is believed to have made it across the border into Mexico or by boat to one of the Central American counties.

Connors is also charged with complicity in the abduction, rape, and murder of the poor little orphan girl spirited away from a Future for Girls Foundation picnic. As I write this, he still awaits separate trial with little chance of acquittal and certainly none of ever again being elected to Congress. Pedophilia is one crime where corruption, as a defense, finds little or no sympathy in the courts.

Erika and Missy's story enabled the Baton Rouge public prosecutor to bring additional charges of slavery against Connors and his father, but political connections being what they are, any serious action against either or both is likely to drag through the courts for years. Public outrage, however, brought support in finding a decent small home in the Baton Rouge suburbs for Missy and her son, and for Erik, a place with a car dealership.

Ashley and Aunt Sarah still reside at Lonsdale Hall. Both were cleared of the horror perpetrated by Freddie and Charlotte as well as the congressman. I've never gone back there and assure you I never will. Its beauty has been totally extinguished for me, though from time to time when in the

South, I visit Felicity in her new assisted-living home, where she happily keeps on painting her beloved flowers, perhaps the only part of my week at that storied plantation house that I will ever care to remember.

And oh! So much for all of them, but what about me? Well, I recovered in a week or so from a bad concussion and a cut scalp and went back home, as planned, on a visit to quite a different family—mine. Gutierrez kindly recommended me to the FBI for a job, but a review board couldn't quite get over my past, which is perhaps just as well. I had suddenly started to feel I'd done my share of police work. What he did do, however, was to join with Tom Whitman in sponsoring me as a free-lance photojournalist. That, with the help, also, of the kindly editor of *Great American Families,* who ended up with a story she never expected, is what I am doing now on my first job as one. Far, far from the Bayou Teche and Lonsdale Hall, as far as I can possibly get and where I learned that beauty often disguises pure evil, I'm covering a yachting regatta at Edgartown on Martha's Vineyard.

End

About the Author

Born to wealth and privilege in New York, David Osborn chose to spurn both as false icons after World War II combat as a Marine Corps dive bomber pilot. On his own and following brief careers in television and public relations, he expatriated to France when falsely accused of un-Americanism in the infamous Senator McCarthy era, paying his way with a co-authored first motion picture script, *Chase a Crooked Shadow*. When its star-studded success took him from laboring in a rock quarry in France into Britain's film industry, he was launched on a long world-class writing career that saw him dangerously engaged during several Cold War years with Czech anticommunist resistance behind the Iron Curtain. Living in France and England as well as isolated for twelve years in a tiny Alpine village in Switzerland, Osborn authored numerous stellar TV plays and a score of major motion pictures, including *The Trap,* which earned an Academy Award nomination. Turning novelist with the critical success of *The Glass Tower* followed by the world best-selling classics *Open Season, The French Decision, Love and Treason,* and a half dozen more outstanding thrillers, he has had many imitators, but none reaching the startling originality of his stories, the stunning impact of his flawless page-turning plots, and his literate prose in each that packs a powerful punch with nearly every line.